Main Street Publishing Presents

Inspirations

The Talent Among Us VII

*Stories and Poems
by Tennessee Writers*

Talent Among Us VII - Inspirations

All rights reserved.
Printed and bound in the United States of America. Except as permitted under the U.S. Copyright Act of 1976: Without limiting the rights under copyright reserved above, no part of this publication may he reproduced, stored in or introduced into a retrieval system, or transmitted, in any form, or by and means (electronic, mechanical. photocopying, recording. or otherwise), without the prior written permission of both the copyright owner and the below publisher of this book.

The publisher does not have any control over and does not assume any responsibility for author or third-party Web sites or their content.

The scanning, uploading, and distribution of this book via the Internet or via any other means without the permission of the author or publisher is illegal and punishable by law. Please purchase only authorized electronic editions, and do not participate in or encourage electronic piracy of copyrighted materials. Your support of the author's rights is appreciated.
*All short-stories and poetry are the property of the writers.

Copyright © 2007
First Edition – First Printing November 2007
Library of Congress Number pending

ISBN # 978-1-934615-10-2
        1-934615-10-2

Published by Main Street Publishing, Inc., Jackson, TN.
Copy Editing by Shari B Hill and Annette W. Galloway
Cover Design by Dr Danny Winbush
Printed and bound by NetPub, Poughkeepsie, NY.

For more information write Main Street Publishing, Inc.,
206 East Main St., Suite 207, P.O. Box 696, Jackson, TN 38302
Phone 1-731-427-7379 or toll free 1-866-457-7379.
E-mail: words@mspbooks.com for managing editor and mspsupport@charterinternet.com for customer service.
Visit us at www.mainstreetpublishing.com and www.mspbooks.com.

Inspirations

A Note from Main Street Publishing

Out of respect for our writers, we have reproduced their works in the same form it was submitted. The views and thoughts of each writer are meant to provoke thought. You may not agree or approve of every poem or short story, but that is your privilege.

The Talent Among Us Began in 2000 with a contest presented by d n english and Dr. Danny Winbush. The contest is held every year with entries from all across West Tennessee. Each volume showcases talented writers from the West Tennessee area.

Table of Contents

Short Stories

Follow The Wind	*Joyce Billingsby*	15
The Secret In The Saddlebags	*Myrlen Britt*	19
Elvis Blues	*Pam Wingo*	28
Ranulf	*Robert A. Caldwell*	32
My Horse Apple Tree And Me	*Betty Jo Loyd Winbush*	40
Play Misty For Me	*Sherry Hughes*	44
Rosie's Baby Ali	*Sherry Hughes*	46
Walks Of Life	*Leah Green*	47
Hand Me Downs	*Kirby Jones*	52
My First Permanent	*Hyla Richardson*	55
Balance Of Chaos	*Maggie Elkins*	58
For Dee	*Maggie Elkins*	60
A Harmonious Discord	*Erin Wyatt*	62
The Meanest Turtle In West Tennessee	*Larry Workman*	65
Just Another Summer Vacation	*Billy Cotner*	68
The Bandit	*Shirley Yockem Barker*	70
Bonnie	*Joyce Corley*	73
Three Little Words	*Donna King*	76
A Ghost Story	*d n english*	79

Poems

"Still Waters"	*Merideth Allyn*	83
Kid Stuff	*Bobby King*	84
"No Saying No"	*Merideth Allyn*	85
Collateral Damage	*Myrlen Britt*	87
My Cedar Chest	*Marilyn McCollum*	88
Nature Reigns @ 2003	*Myrtle D. Russell*	90
The Minister's Wife Poems	*Robert A. Caldwell*	93
Grandmartha's Overnight Visitor	*Martha McNatt*	100
Country Raisin'	*Cousin Tuny*	104

Fallowed Ground	*Gary Kirk*	*103*
Goofy Words	*Bobby King*	*105*
Let Waters Flow @2007	*Myrtle D. Russell*	*106*
Marriage	*Joyce Billingsby*	*108*
Memory Games	*Martha McNatt*	*109*
What If ???	*Bobby King*	*110*
A Friend Is...	*Bobby King*	*111*
(I Got) A Taste Of Heaven	*Mark Kendrick*	*112*
Teacakes And Soda Water	*Kimberly S. Morris*	*114*
Nectar Of Jazz	*Kimberly S. Morris*	*116*
"The Storm"	*JAEL*	*117*
I Am	*L.B. Sloane*	*118*
Suzanne	*JAEL*	*119*
If Life Were Easy	*Beverley Kay Matlock*	*121*
In A Child's Eyes	*Beverley Kay Matlock*	*122*
"Great-grandmother"	*Katherine Haney Williams*	*123*
"Morning Prayers"	*Katherine Haney Williams*	*124*
Beautiful Mosaic	*Leah Green*	*126*
A Garden And A Woman	*Frankie Woody*	*127*
Weeping Wisteria	*Frankie Woody*	*128*
The Horse Apple Tree	*Dr. Danny O. Winbush*	*129*
The Shadow	*Sheila Love Nicholson*	*130*
Two Apples	*Thomas Aud*	*131*
Man-made Mornings	*Thomas Aud*	*132*
Only Once In A Life-time	*Dr. Clementine G. "Glem" Spencer*	*133*
Life	*Hyla Richardson*	*134*
Me, Myself And I	*Cassie McGill*	*135*
Joy.Music Of The Soul	*Dory Lamb*	*136*
A Stitch In Time	*Dory Lamb*	*137*
Let The Bells Ring Loud	*Erin Wyatt*	*138*
Shivering On A Mountaintop	*Sula Hillhouse*	*139*
Our Promised Land	*Sula Hillhouse*	*140*
A Man Was Reaching For Coffee . . .	*David Strait*	*141*
Birds? Sure, I've Got Shelves Full.	*David Strait*	*142*
Never Forgotten	*Jeremy Elkins*	*143*
Tonight And Forever	*Jeremy Elkins*	*145*

Introduction
by David Strait

    The genres of short fiction and poetry seem to hover in a state of flux at the outskirts of mainstream literature. At present, we can walk into a bookshop in any given airport across the country and find the exact same best-selling novels, memoirs, and self-help titles. In large chain bookstores, the stacks of poetry are dwarfed by the travel, teen-lit, and inspirational sections. This is not to say that best sellers are poor reading. It is not to slight books on travel or personal development. It does prompt us to ask, however, where the more traditional genres of poetry and short fiction fit into the world of contemporary literature. Also, with the ever-increasing global nature of trade, both commercial trade and the free exchange of ideas and information online, another question arises. What relevance does regional literature sustain in context of an audience that keeps the whole world as close as the nearest computer?

    Over the past fifty years, short fiction has served as either a launch pad or an experiment lab for writers who are primarily novelists. This is changing. There was a time, within the past century, when writers made money and created a reputation based on the publication of their short stories in national periodicals. Hemingway and Fitzgerald serve as examples. As recently as Salinger's *Franny and Zooey*, originally published as two separate entries in *The New Yorker*, a major author's next short story was eagerly anticipated. Fiction drove a high volume of sales for many publications. Now the popularity of the short story is waxing again, after a half-century lull. We see this in the likes of Benjamin Percy, who has created quite a buzz with his 2006 collection *The Language of Elk* and his Pushcart Prize-winning story *Refresh, Refresh*. Anthony Doerr's *The Shell Collector*, also a book of short stories, has received critical acclaim equaling or surpassing the response to his longer prose. It is not surprising, in a fast-paced society intent on multi-tasking and elevator pitches, that our attention spans are trending toward *After the Ball*, as opposed to *Anna Karenina*.

In the September 2006 volume of *Poetry*, John Barr challenges, with leveling force, 21st century writers. In the essay *American Poetry in the New Century*, Barr remarks that, "A new poetry becomes necessary not because we want one, but because the way poets have learned to write no longer captures the way things are, how things have changed." In September of 2007, also within the pages of *Poetry*, Brian Phillips gives a nod to Barr's observations. He begs to differ, though, offering a "Problem of taste" as the bane of contemporary readers and writers of poetry.

These are two examples among many. Critics, and poets themselves, are ever finding or inventing reasons that poetry is a dead or dying art form. It seems to be a badge of courage adopted by writers, as if a lack of audience will insure the reward of some sought-after martyrdom. I've heard MFA faculty members bemoan the fact that "too many people are writing poetry, and not enough people are reading it." This is a skewed view. It is true that there are boundless opportunities for writers, both beginning and established, to publish in small journals or on web sites. It is true that volumes of poetry rarely see the degree of financial success that accompanies a best-selling novel. Poetry is a different animal, though. Its audience, for the most part, isn't comprised of those satisfied with the role of spectator. Poetry's followers are eager to engage in the universal conversation of their art, both listening and speaking. With fingers positioned correctly on the pulse, we find that, in fact, poetry is alive and thriving.

An argument rages. It is highlighted in the 2007 November/December issue of *Poets & Writers*: the contest system or the series model? How do the big publishers find and select the best new candidates for print? Did I hear someone mention a reality TV show? We can flip through hundreds of channels on the tube, have movies delivered to our homes, or find almost any book title from anywhere in the world with the help of simple search engines. Has regional literature succumbed to the small world getting smaller? It hasn't. Instead, with so much information so easily accessible, audiences are hungry for something that feels personal. We are drowning in things, and starving for humanity. Regional literature still provides this human connection for which there is no replacement. Local authors can take heart that, like poetry, our regional literature is alive and well.

Criticism and commentary aside, as a past contributor to the annual Talent Among Us publication, I am excited to be part of a community of writers who are eager to create and share. With short stories making a comeback, poetry retaining its relevance, and regional literature filling an important social niche, West Tennessee writers move forward through the following pages, creating a vibrant body of work one word, one line, at a time.

Short Stories

1st Place Short Story Co-Winners

1st Place

FOLLOW THE WIND

Joyce Billingsby

April had not seen him in twenty years, and she had never seen him dressed in a suit. She thought he had aged harshly, deeply etched lines were carved across his forehead, and his dark luxurious hair showed touches of gray. Those wonderful lips always curved in a smile were rigid, angry, unrelenting. Just like the last time she saw him. When the call came from Chicago looking for next of kin, she felt a torrent of emotions cascading across her numbed soul. Memories painfully locked away that appeared at forbidden times, almost overpowering her with passion and despair.

After she called him to her apartment that night to tell him she was marrying his twin brother, he had never been heard from since, simply vanishing from the face of the world. Where had he lived? Surely he had found someone to love, but there were no survivors listed. Killed in a barroom brawl, was this a synopsis of his life? If she had chosen him instead, what kind of life would they have lived? He was endowed with a reckless wild spirit, humor filling his soul, his rich laughter bouncing off the wind. Had his dream also died the night he had left her weeping, or had he found flashes of the rainbow leading him onward to that mythical pot of gold? What had brought him to this tragic lonely end?

They had argued that last night, tearfully and angrily.

He had looked at her incredulously when she made her declaration, "But you love me," he said in disbelief. "We've planned a life together. How can you tell me you love my brother more?"

"I'm so sorry, Farron," she wept. "I didn't mean this to happen

– but I just know Darron is right for me. I've decided I want to spend the rest of my life with him."

"We were going to travel and see the world," he cried in despair; "follow the wind, camp out at night beneath the stars, and love each other forever. I won't let you do this," he cried in desperation. His deep brown eyes were filled with pain, his handsome face filled with anguish. For a moment she wavered; what had seemed so right a few moments ago now left her reeling with indecision.

"Those were just romantic daydreams," she whispered desperately. "I want a home, a family. I need security in my life. I grew up poor and unwanted, shifted from one relative's house to another. I want a stable life. Please try to understand. Darron will give me what I need."

His hands reached for her brusquely, crushing her against his chest. She felt his heart pounding against her face. "This is what you need," he cried hoarsely, his lips forcing hers open beneath his. She felt the familiar fire spreading through her veins as she struggled vainly against him. "This is what you want."

"Please," she begged. "I've made up my mind. I know I'm doing the right thing. Nothing you can say or do will change my mind. You must try to understand."

"Then let me give you a wedding present you will never forget," he said hoarsely. Was it anger at her rejection or pain from his loss that drove his hunger? Her pleas were silenced beneath her own growing passion, and she felt herself weakening beneath his relentless power. "And every time he makes love to you, remember me."

And God help her, she had. Tears brimmed her eyes as she stood staring at his still body. She had traded a life of spontaneity, passion, and exuberance for a life of safety, mediocrity — and regret. Darron had stayed on the family farm and their lives had been governed by the crops — planting, harvesting, harvesting, and planting. And the glory years of her life had slipped mundanely away.

Her daughter moved to her side staring down at this unknown stranger. Amy, the sunshine of her world, was leaving for college this fall, and already April dreaded the loneliness that would come with the absence of her friend and dearest companion. Amy would happily leave her home, unaware that the careless decisions she made now would alter the course of her life forever and affect the lives of those around her. She would make choices without the guidance and protection of her loving parents. Adults should have a second chance to get it right, April thought achingly. Why must one be penalized for the rest of their life for stubborn decisions made in their youth?

Her husband was courteously biding farewell to neighbors who had come to the funeral home, paying their respects to this returning prodigal son. Amy slipped her hand through her mother's arm. Her black hair tumbled riotously over her shoulders as her dark eyes stared fearfully at this unknown relative, her happy carefree demeanor subdued by this unwelcome picture of death.

April suddenly recalled one early spring when she and little Amy had run up the hillside to gather yellow buttercups growing profusely in the edge of the field. Buffeted by the wind, their hair blowing wildly against their faces, they had staggered backward in the ferocious gusts, laughing and shouting with joy. "Mama, Mama," Amy cried ecstatically; "the wind is telling us which way to go!"

"He looks so much like Daddy, it's frightening," Amy whispered in awe. "I keep thinking —what if that was my daddy lying in that coffin?"

With tears in her eyes, April turned slowly to her daughter unable to utter the words she could now admit to herself. It was not Amy's father lying in the coffin — it was Amy's mother! Killing the heart so the mind can live is suicide, and April would have escaped that slow tortuous death years ago if only she had followed the wind now silenced forever.

BIO

Joyce Billingsby is a farm wife and grandmother and resides in Weakley County. Her novel "Wildwood: Confessions of a Moon Wife" has been released. A short story called "Mountain Wife" will appear in Muscadine Lines: A Southern Journal in the Sept-Oct edition. A new novel "Song of Elizabeth" will be published later this year.

1st Place

The Secret in the Saddlebags
Myrlen Britt

I was ten years old on July twenty first 1945. It's one birthday I'll never forget. A grizzled old cowboy and a worn out old horse changed my life forever.

Momma and my sister were frying chicken and making an apple pie for my birthday dinner and had sent me to the garden to pull some onions, cucumbers and tomatoes. It hadn't rained in several days and the earth was so dry that each step made the dust swirl around my ankles. The soles of my feet were tough as leather from going barefoot all summer so, I never paid much attention to the hot earth. It was a Saturday and as usual my dad and older brothers were in Lexington, the county seat. They would bring home ice and all the fixings for ice cream.

The cotton crop had been laid by and school wouldn't begin for a week then let out again in six weeks for us to pick the cotton. I was looking forward to a week of fishing and playing softball with my friends. "Hey boy coulda ol' man get a fresh drank of water?" The voice belonged to a man with a wrinkled face riding a horse that looked like it was on its last leg.

I had been so intent on pulling cucumbers and thinking about fried chicken and ice cream I hadn't heard him come down the dirt road. It was impossible to tell his age.

He and his horse were covered with dust and sweat ran down his face creating streaks of mud. I noticed that his damp, matted hair was snow white but there was still a twinkle in his blue eyes that belied his age.

"Yessir, come on over to the back porch we got fresh water there," I knew my dad would do the same thing.

"How 'bout ol' Chisum here, it's been a long time since I watered him"

"We got a pond over yonder by th' barn, I'll water him for you." I volunteered.

"That's mighty kind of you, boy," he climbed down from the old saddle pulling two weather worn saddle bags with him and went up onto the back porch. His step was surprisingly spry. He filled the dipper and emptied it in seconds. He drank another dipper full then filling it a third time he stepped to the edge of the porch and threw the water in his face.

He crossed the yard still carrying the saddle bags as though they were filled with gold and joined me at the pond, the horse drank his fill and I led him to the Elm tree by the barn tying the reins to a limb where he could cool off in the shade.

"It's kind of you to lend a helping' hand to an' ol' man, sonny boy."

"Well, that's what my dad would want me to do."

"Where you from, mister?"

"I guess you could say I'm from all over, sonny, most recently Arkansas, been choppin' cotton in th' Delta, not far from Memphis."

"That's hard work for an ol..I mean, choppin'..uh.. cotton is..uh…."

He laughed and cut me off, "you was gonna say hard work for an' ol' man."

I felt my face burn and knew it had to be blood red, "I, I'm sorry, mister, it's just that…." I didn't know what to say.

He patted me gently on the shoulder and said "forget it, if I had a dollar fer every time I stuck my foot in my mouth I'd be richer'n Rockefeller."

At that moment I knew I had a new friend. My momma's daddy died before I was born and I was never close to my other granddad and it felt good getting approval from an older person.

"You hungry, mister?" I asked as my way of apologizing.

"Well, ol' Chisum ain't eat all day, but I'm fine."

"I'll get him some corn an' then momma'll make you something."

"I don't want to be no trouble, sonny boy, you done enough already."

"My dad would skin me if I didn't tell momma you was hungry, come on in th' house."

He reluctantly followed me inside removing the old cowboy style hat. I reached for the saddle bags to put them on a chair but he gripped them even tighter and pulled them away. Momma had her hands full of biscuit dough for the pie crust when we entered the kitchen but she never batted an eye. She was used to my dad picking up strays and we were always willing to share the little bit we had.

"Well, well, what have we got here young'un?"

"Him and his horse Chisum were thirsty and hungry, Momma, I fed Chisum some corn but he's hungry," pointing at the stranger.

Momma told him her name then mine and sister's and asked, "What are you called, sir?"

"My name's William McCarty, ma'am, folks who git to know me usually call me Uncle Will.

Momma smiled that sweet smile and said, "I'm a trifle old to call you uncle, Mr. McCarty, but the young'uns might like to, seein' they don't have a lot of kinfolks 'cept their daddy and me."

She heated up some cold biscuits and fat back bacon from breakfast and cooked him some eggs and made fresh coffee. He was too polite to wolf his food down but I could tell it had been a long time since his last good meal. He kept going back to the jar of homemade muscadine jam and smearing it onto a biscuit. All the while he would stop eating for a moment and reach under his chair to check on the saddlebags. I thought he must have something pretty important in those bags the way he kept checking on them.

It wasn't long before dad and my brothers got home, I seen dad with something in a brown sack head to the barn and just for a moment allowed myself to dream about the Daisy air-rifle like I'd seen in the Sears Roebuck wish book every Christmas.

My brothers said hello to "Uncle" Will and started on the homemade ice-cream; dad came in looking like he was hiding something, he never could keep a secret when it come to buying us kids presents but he sure was trying to hold something in. I knew then I was going to get that air rifle.

It didn't take long for Uncle Will to warm up to dad and by suppertime they had already agreed he would stay with us and help bring in the cotton crop, until then he would help mend fences, sharpen plow points for next spring and begin cutting wood for winter heat and for momma's wood burning range. I was so excited about having a substitute grandpa I hardly remember how the chicken tasted. But the ice cream was a different story; we didn't get it as often as fried chicken.

"Will, we don't have a lot of room in th' house so, the best we can do is a cot in the tool shed,' my dad hated for him to have to sleep in the barn but it was actually cooler in summer than the house.

"After some of my sleepin' arrangements durin' th' Lincoln County war in New Mexico I can sleep on broke glass."

"I remember my great uncle talkin' 'bout them range wars, but I never really believed they happened and you say you was there?" said dad.

"Uh-huh, I shore was."

"Why, you couldn'tve been more'n a child," my mother said.

"Yes ma'am, I was jist a slip of a boy but we growed up fast in them days."

He began to ask about the crops and such and it was clear he didn't want to remember anymore about those days, at least not just then. All that changed over the next six months as he and I became best friends. He began to open up more about his cowboying days when we were alone. He'd always say, "no sense in telling' your maw, sonny, women are more delicate than men, she don't need to hear 'bout no killin'; guess we'd all be better off if they wasn't no killin'." He'd stare off into space like he was re-living something that happened sixty years before. Then he'd pick up a cedar board and begin carving something for me. He could carve any kind of animal from cedar. I still have his crowning achievement, a six gun that looked real after he painted it black. I just wish I had all the contents from his saddlebags but a tornado in '47 destroyed a piece of American history. But I'm getting ahead of myself.

One day during one of our man/boy bonding sessions he began to talk about the famous gunslingers he had either known or had seen in his rowdy youth during the eighteen seventies and early eighties.

"Ever heard of Billy the Kid?" he asked out of the blue.

"Course I have, ain't everybody?" "He killed twenty one men before Pat Garrett killed him when he was just twenty one years old, that's a dead man for each of his years." I was proud of my knowledge of that famous gunfighter.

"Sonny boy, I've learned one lesson for sure in almost eighty three year of livin', don't believe half of what you hear and even less of what you read."

He went back to scraping the barrel of my six shooter with a piece of broken glass, making it as smooth as fine grain sandpaper would.

"Did you ever see Billy the Kid?" I wasn't ready to let it go.

"I rode with him, he never killed no twenty one men, probably not more'n six and I know for a fact four of them needed killin'." He stopped abruptly as though he had said too much.

"Golly, you rode with Billy the Kid?" I was so excited I almost wet my pants.

"Ain't nothing' to be proud of, sonny boy, ain't nothing' to be proud of."

Then he grinned, "I never did feel bad 'bout takin' a few of ol' John Chisum's cows, though."

I suddenly realized why he'd named his old horse Chisum, it was his way of remembering something amusing from his youth. He stopped working and laid the unfinished gun down and walked outside the corncrib where he worked when the weather was damp.

"Think ol' Chisum needs to stretch his legs, we'll be back in time for supper." He got the saddle and saddle bags from the tool shed and put the bridle in Chisum's mouth.

He struggled to mount him and for the first time I realized just how old eighty two was.

Uncle Will had just about come to his end and it made me want to cry.

That night after supper he lit his lantern and headed out the door to his quarters. It was a clear, cold January night and he was bundled up in a flannel shirt and long fleeced lined jumper. Dad had bought him a Warm Morning wood stove that kept his room nice and warm. He had invested in an Aladdin lamp so he could work on his carvings at night since the lantern didn't give enough light. I had at least one of every animal he had ever seen including an Armadillo that he remembered from his days long ago in Texas. But he kept carving them every minute he wasn't working.

He reached the kitchen door and turned and motioned for me with his hand. I followed him outside where the full moon was reflecting off the hoar frost and the frozen pond. It was so still with no wind, it was sort of spooky; he began to speak, "Sonny, your family has been mighty good to ol' Will an' I'll never forget it, you an' me are buds like some of my buds a long time ago."

"I like having you here, Uncle Will."

"I'm gonna tell you something' nobody on earth knows but me an' th' good Lord, even if some jackleg writers and so-called historians think they do, but I want you to promise not to tell anyone, even your family as long as I'm alive."

My lips begin to quiver and I thought I was going to cry.

"Promise?"

"Of course I do if that's what you want, but what is it?" I hung onto every word the old man spoke.

"Pat Garrett was a decent man an' a good sheriff," he began.

"But he killed his friend, Billy Bonney."

"Remember what I tol' you about believing' everything you read?"

I nodded my head, "uh huh."

"Well, this is the truth of the matter, Pat helped fake Billy's death and let him escape after Governor Lew Wallace pardoned him!" "They ain't nothin' in that grave but a rotted coffin filled with rocks and cactus."

"I read that Governor Wallace went back on his word and had Billy hunted down and killed by Garrett in the Maxwell ranch house." I was totally confused. I was an avid reader of paper back westerns and most purported to be true stories of the wild west and now here was Uncle Will, who I really respected, saying something entirely different.

"Sonny, go over there an' git them saddlebags from under my cot."

They were so heavy I had to drag them across the floor, "what's in here, Uncle Will?"

"Ain't gonna tell you jist now, sonny, but I want you to have everything in 'em after I'm gone." "I will tell you this much though, Governor Wallace give Billy one of the first copies of Ben Hur that he wrote, along with a full pardon, believe it or not Billy loved to read."

"You ain't goin' nowhere are you, Uncle Will, you have a home here as long as you live," the words stuck in my throat as I said "as long as you live."

He pulled me to him and hugged me like he had never done before and I saw tears welling up in his eyes.

'Time runs out for everybody sooner or later, sonny an' mine is about gone."

"You know th' Indians used to know when it was time to leave the earth and go to the hunting ground in the sky, they'd jist go off in th' woods alone and die, that ain't a bad way to go, sonny boy, I've had a long life and most of it has been good, but the past few months have been th' best, mostly 'cause of you." He continued to hold me in his grip.

He finally let go and wiping his eyes on his shirt sleeve he said gruffly, "you run along now, it's past yore bedtime and yore daddy'll be out here lookin' for you."

I walked slowly across the barn yard listening to the hoarfrost crunch under my feet. Looking up into the deep black sky I thought about the moon and all those same stars that I was looking at had been shining on Uncle Will in New Mexico over sixty years ago. I had a strange premonition that this was the last time I would see Uncle Will; I began to cry.

The following morning Uncle Will wasn't at the table when I came into the kitchen, my dad had a strange look on his face. "Children, I know how much ya'll had come to think of Will, specially you, he motioned at me, we all kinda got used to havin' him here but I'm afraid he won't be comin' back."

"Why, Dad?" I cried out.

"I took Will to th' doctor in Lexington last week and he found some growths in his throat and his stomach is about eat up with what looks like cancer, th' kind that can't be treated, this morning I went to check on him and he's gone, so is Chisum, I'm sorry, kids."

I left the table without touching my eggs and biscuits and ran out the door to the tool shed. Once inside I looked under his bed and there was the saddle bags. I could barely see how to undo the leather straps through my tears but I had to know what he was trying to tell me the night before. The first bag had an old six-shooter wrapped in oily cloths along with some yellowed newspaper clippings about some of the daring things Billy the Kid had been accused of doing. There was also some copies of Shakespeare and on the inside was written:

"To my good friend, Billy, best regards, signed, Major Tunstall."

I slowly opened the other bag and found a very old copy of Ben Hur, I opened it to the fly leaf and there in faded ink was an inscription;

To William Bonney, called Billy the Kid, thank you for being a young man of honor, sincerely, Lew Wallace: New Mexico Territorial Governor.

Inside the book was a piece of parchment paper that was so fragile with age I was almost afraid to touch it. I managed to get the book open where it lay and read:

"To all men present, let it be known that by the authority vested in me as Governor of the Territory of New Mexico I, hereby grant a full pardon to one William Bonney McCarty known also as Billy the Kid. I further restore all rights and privileges of citizenship to the above mentioned."

We never learned of Uncle Will's, I mean Billy's fate but many years later bone fragments of a large animal and a human were found in the heavily wooded area between the Cumberland and Tennessee rivers. My family felt like it had to be Billy the Kid and his horse, Chisum.

Later that day I showed everything to my family then put it back in the saddlebags and hid it under my bed. For the next two years I would take the items out and look at them as I tried to visualize Uncle Will as a young cowboy and gunfighter. Sadly, a tornado destroyed our home in nineteen forty seven along with all the evidence left behind by Billy the Kid.

BIO

While Myrlen has lived in three states and seven cities his heart remains in West Tennessee. He shares his life with wife Faye and enjoys his three children and five grand children. He is presently working on Volume IV of his Taproot Series Titled "Golden Memories."

2nd Place Winner

ELVIS BLUES
Pam Wingo

    Yesterday was a long time ago, yet sometimes it flashes before me and makes me shudder just like a snake at my feet, coiled and ready to strike right at that moment. Now, I laugh about that day that's frozen in time, but trust me, it wasn't so funny then! Snake bites, of one kind or another, can stay with ya for sometime and the repercussions can hit you like a ton of bricks over and over again.......if you let em!

    Jack and Gin loved their little songs they played on their red record player. The nursery rhymes would be so fondly listened to over and over again until they had them all memorized. The precious twosome would dance and sing off key so loudly just to outdo the other. One happy morning Jack and Ginger found some old boxes under the stairs that I hadn't gone through in years. They were delighted when they came to one filled with black, small discs....my old 45 record collection. Most had the Motown label but a few had RCA and the name of Elvis Presley. OH MY GOSH, my heart started to flutter as the three of us ran to the little red player. We wiggled, we squealed with delight, and I fell in love all over again, at the same time my four and five year old discovered THE KING OF ROCK n ROLL!

    This was sure a far cry from the nursery rhymes! No more Baa Baa Black Sheep! All Jack, Gin and their Alright Mama wanted now was to hear from the REAL BLACK SHEEP himself.....Elvis Presley!!!!! So, we hopped into the car and made a mad dash for the Record Shop in The Village. Walking into the place was like walking into a concert. It was poster filled and giant cardboard likenesses stood right before us. There HE was, posed in a tight white jumpsuit, blue suede shoes, with sunglasses as big as the moon. Each child ran to him screamin, "is dis him," "is dis EVIS"?

Suddenly, out of nowhere, there stood this tall, slim, red-haired salesgirl. She had obviously been watchin us from afar, just waitin to strike a Heartbreak Hotel on us! All sweet and gooey she said, "Whachal little people need?" I could swear she was also including me! And you know how intuition just makes ya shiver sometimes, well, the blonde hairs on my head practically stood on end! I immediately knew that Red, the Viper, was not wantin to sell us Elvis records!!! This tall Carrot-top was Our Enemy! I was overtaken with the GI blues!!!!!

My Suspicious Mind was racin as Jack and Gin went about happily looking through the Spinnin Disc Shop. Sure enough, the Scarlet Harlot bent down and whispered, "You are Roberts wife, right?" I wanted to answer, "No, I'm just the housekeeper and babysitter," but darn, I was too curious!!! This was a new one! "I really need to talk to you," Red proceeded to hiss. I looked straight into those cold dark eyes, paid for Elvis, and said, "Sure, that will be a real treat....how about 2;00?" I knew my two Hound Dogs would be worn out by then.

Lunch with the King was awesome....we rocked, we rolled, we shimmied, we shook like something on a fuzzy tree, and we sang until naptime when I had to face the 'Bob Thing'.

Sure enough, the phone rang at 2:00 on the nose. I sat speechless as I listened to the venomous tales the Copperheaded Queen was spittin into my ear! It seems Red and her family were involved in a lawsuit, hired Bob to solve their problems, and fallen IN LOVE WITH THE SNAKE-IN-THE-GRASS!!!! How romantic!!! I mean the whole family was infatuated with the charmin low-life. Scaly Reds parents also entered the phone conversation and informed me of Bobs undying love for their offspring. They couldn't wait for him to become their son-in-law since, "you'll will be divorcing soon anyway, right?", said Mother Serpent. They were tickled pink to soon be, "havin' a lawya in the family," said Daddy Reptile!

True, there had been no Peace in our Valley for sometime, but I wasn't about to let THEM know. I thanked these lovely home wrecking Vipers for the enlightening conversation, then just sat mesmerized.

If adultery was a crime, All the jailhouses would be rockin with BOBS!

Oh, Daddy, Daddy was sure gonna be cryin tonight! That is, if he managed to SLITHER home.

TIPS:
Always have a defense ready, like a good heavy rake or Moth Balls when vermin invade your territory. Listen to any Elvis record right now and you'll be in love in seconds!

BIO

"ELVIS BLUES" is my favorite, true short story I wrote as part of my co-authored book, "COOKIN' FOR BOB," forty tales of unsavory relationships, marriage, and divorce.

As a born, raised, and educated Memphis, Tennessean, I, like so many others, had several real-life "Elvis Encounters." Every year, around the honored date of Elvis' death and somewhat resurrection, my now-grown children and I just love reminiscing about all of the great "Hound Dog" stuff. I guess now we'll have to include the reading of "ELVIS BLUES" as part of our yearly celebration and journey through time.

I am presently and guess always will be, a retired 33 year Biology teacher who refuses to accept retirement as a time to sit back and let time take its toll! Writing is just another one of my expressions of fulfilling the dreams I never made time for…watch out world, here I come!

3rd Place Co-Winners

3rd Place Winner
Ranulf
Robert A. Caldwell

"Don't be going this day, Father. Tis' an evil day to be away."

"Nay, Aleward. I'll let no superstition keep me from the bishop's business," said the tall young priest. "Now bestir your lazy arse and saddle the roan. Forget not my heavy cloak and a flagon of wine."

"Will ye be gone the night, Father?" asked the groom.

"The night, good Aleward? Nay, for I must say mass on the morrow. Tis All Saint's Day."

'Tis not All Saints Day I fear, Father, but the eve of the day. The spirits that walk abroad……"

"Enough of your sapistry, you rogue! Fetch my horse! I'll not face the bishop's displeasure. The fear of faeries will not line his greedy pockets."

The morning was warm in the last days of October, as the tall young priest left the abbey courtyard and cantered down the dusty road. Although he rode alone, he did not fear outlaws, for he was deep chested and powerfully built. A broad sword and buckler hung to one side of his saddle, and a pouch containing priestly vestments to the other. Indeed, his bearing was more that of the soldier than a priest, but priest he was, like his Norman father before him. The church offered education and advancement, and he had been quick to grasp both. His clever mind and gifts of administration brought him to the attention of the bishop of Durham, who made Ranulf his clerk, sagely observing that the young priest was far better suited to the counting table than to altar and confessional. Indeed, Ranulf's fondness was for drinking, wenching, and wrestling rather than for devotional reading and the veneration of holy relics. A secular priest he was, with a booming laugh not meant to echo through monastic halls.

Ranulf rode on for an hour, until he was only two miles from the village of Burcwen. His horse was soaked with sweat, so he turned from the old Roman highway and headed toward a large copse of trees. Beyond lay a large, deep pond, renowned for a huge fish said to swim in its depths. A keen fisherman, Ranulf lamented his lack of pole, hook and line. At least he could water his tired horse and slake his own thirst from the flagon of wine hanging from his saddle. He urged his horse on and soon emerged from the trees to see the pond ahead. Smelling the water, the horse trotted to the water's edge and bent to drink. Ranulf lifted his flagon to his lips and took a deep draught. Wiping his mouth, he suddenly noticed how still the air was and how very cool. He could not hear the singing of birds nor the peeping of frogs. Suddenly, the silence was broken as he heard the soft laughter of a girl.

Startled, Ranulf turned in his saddle to behold a young woman perched on a fallen log at the pond's edge. She was cooling her bare feet in the water. An astonishing mane of dark red hair cascaded to her waist. Still amazed, Ranulf quickly looked from left to right.

"Have no fear, Father Ranulf," she said in a lilting voice. "No one will leap at you from the pond's depth!"

"By Jesu, so you know my name," he replied uneasily. "How so?"

"All in the shire know of the priest who stands a head taller than other men, and serves the greed of the bishop of Durham. And who does not wear the tonsure nor trim his hair in the Norman way. 'Tis said you know your fat master's account books better than King David knew the psalms!'

"How now, lass! What know you of King David and the psalter? Know you your catechism? And by the foreskin of Moses, you are impudent to speak such of men in holy orders!"

"Know I of King David that he sought the wife of his captain Uriah and caused him to die on the battlefield. That he was mighty in battle and in bed, for he frightened to death the fool Nabal that he might take Abigail as wife. That he played the lyre and wrote the psalms, of them being one hundred and fifty. Yea, know I the catechism, yet little I care for it mumbled by the stinking breath of old priests. And your master the lord bishop, does he not love his wife of gold and his mistress of silver even the more than he loves his daughters, mutton and ale?"

"Sweet Jesu, how you do talk, lass!" exclaimed Ranulf. "Pray tell who taught you letters?"

"My own father taught me, Sir Priest, " she said proudly. "He is the notary of Bercwen."

"And taught you well, I see," laughed Ranulf. "and yea, my lord bishop doth dearly love both trencher and treasury! But tell me, lass, did your dear father teach you to catch fish with your pretty toes as bait? For did he, I fear his table will be bare tonight!"

"No, Sir Priest. I came here seeking berries. I stepped in nettles and would wash away their sting, for 'tis sharp!"

"What are you called, lass?" asked Ranulf suddenly.

"I hight Maeve," she said simply.

"Maeve." 'Tis not a name one hears. 'Tis not Norman, nor Saxon, and I think not Pictish."

"Tis Irish. It was my mother's mother's name, " she said wistfully.

"Ah, Maeve," said Ranulf gently, seeing her sadness. "Howbeit that a notary of Bercwen took an Irish wife?"

"When my mother was a child, she was stolen from her people. My father bought her from a ship's captain when she was twelve summers. He came to love her and took her to wife."

"Your father is an educated man. Did he teach her letters as well?"

"No, Sir Priest. She cared not a whit for such learning. My mother was creature of the woods and fens. She could read the signs of forest, streams and fens as my father would read a book.

She took her learning from the bees and the cows. My father said she was fey."

"And does your good mother now live? Have you sisters or brothers?

"A fever took her two summers ago," she said sadly. "And there is no one but my father and me now. But come. Will you pick berries with me? Come stain your mouth with the juice of wild berries……..with me."

"Indeed I will, lass," said Ranulf as he swung from his horse with surprising ease for his bulk. "If only to protect you from the nettles."

After he tied his horse to a tree, Ranulf looked in vain for the girl. She had disappeared. "What work of the devil is this," he muttered, hurriedly crossing himself. He then heard her tinkling laugh, and saw her peeking at him from a thicket. "Are you of the faerie folk, to appear and disappear at will?" he asked.

"Aye," she said, "some will say that. But I misdoubt I cause fear in a man like you."

For a quarter of an hour, Ranulf pursued the girl through the woods, her gentle, mocking laugh just ahead of him. When he came upon her underneath a great oak, her gown was gone and she stood before him, naked with the glory of Eve. Her body was golden curves and shadows, splashed with dark red under arms and belly. As he stood before her, he saw that her oval eyes were deep green with flecks of gold. As he spread his cloak for them beneath the mistletoe laden oak, he knew that he had never seen eyes so green nor kissed a mouth so sweet.

"I am your first man," he said quietly.

"Yes you are, my love."

"Why lass, you've scarce known me an hour," Ranulf said carefully, half fearing that she might disappear as quickly as she has come into his life. "And you gave yourself to me."

"My father is old, and you are held to be a man of ambition," she said levelly. "And I will be so good for you," she whispered, clamping her wide mouth on his.

As they lay together, he began to speak to her earnestly. A priest could marry, as his father had.

Even the lord bishop had his woman, a plump, jolly launderess who slipped into his bed at night. Ranulf would speak to her father at once. She demured about riding into the village with him. It would cause the townfolk to gossip and would cause her father much embarrassment. They agreed that he would go to her father and ask for her. Father Godrith, the priest of Bercwen was well known to Ranulf, and he would marry them in a fortnight.

As he rode away, Ranulf could not take his eyes off the beautiful girl as she stood by the pond and waved. He ducked to dodge a low hanging branch, and when he looked back, she was gone.

"Sapristi!" he exclaimed. "She must indeed be of the faerie folk, for I am truly bewitched." He thought of how her strong arms enfolded him as she pulled him down into her softness, her cloak of dark red hair wrapping about him as a net. An immensely practical man, he reflected with approval on her answers. She had said that she was of sixteen summers, with an old father. And Ranulf admitted the ambition that burned like a coal in his breast. It will be a good match, he thought. She is the daughter of a respected man of law. And he would awaken no more in a cold abbey to the sound of sleepy priests mumbling their morning office.

Ranulf rode into Bercwen and sought the church. The bishop's business first, he thought, and then to seek Maeve's father. At the church, he found the priest, Father Godrith, distributing alms.

"Ho, Father Ranulf!" cried the older priest. "Alight from your horse and drink new ale with me! You look as if the horse rode *you* from Durham!"

The two priests strolled to the garden behind the church, and Ranulf collapsed on a bench. A buxom servant girl brought ale, bread and cheese, winking at Ranulf as she set his tankard before him.

"Surely you come bringing the bishop's blessing and will return taking his tithe,' teased Father Godrith. "Now my son, tell me news of Durham. The good bishop continues to wax fatter and richer, that I know. Does old Brother Ethelred still live, or has fasting and penance claimed his miserable life at last? Did Father Ambrosius get cured of the wen on his nose? The nose he was always shoving in other's business?"

"Patience, patience, Father, and I will surely tell all. But I must first speak to you of matters more urgent to me. Know you the notary of Bercwen?"

"Sweet Jesu, young Ranulf! Him I know indeed! In a village so small and miserable as this, I know when every man and woman swyve and when every babe breaks wind! Indeed know I the notary. A sad man. He comes much to the saying of the divine office."

"Ah," said Ranulf. "A pious man then, for he prays for the soul of his dead wife."

"And of his daughter, as well. Here, have more ale."
"What say you, Father?" cried Ranulf, gripping the old priest's arm with fingers of steel.

"Do you not know, my son? The notary's daughter drowned a year ago this very day, "T'was on the eve of All Saint's Day. The day the Woads call Samhain. Gurth, the smith found her when he took his sons to fish. He thought mayhap she went to the pond to bathe, and caught her long hair on the roots of a tree. Ranulf! Are you ill my son?"

"Father," whispered Ranulf, "will you hear my confession?"

37

"Look ye," said the old woman to her friends, "there rides the bishop's man. Surely he has come to squeeze his fat master's portion from the coffers of Father Godrith."

"Eeeeehhh," said old Mag to her companions as they sat and combed wool. "From the pale looks of him, he needs a good woman to wed and to bed. "Twill make his cheeks glow, Alya! And have ye not granddaughters?"

"Aye, but he's gentry and will want to marry a highborn lady. Besides, know ye not the rede that old Father Wulf would quote: **"Whoever would bed an unmarried virgin on All Saint's Day Eve, his name shall become a curse."** 'Tis the day of Samhain."

1. From the *Encyclopedia Britannica of 1911*:

Ranulf Flambard or Ralph (d. 1128) was Bishop of Durham and Lord Chancellor (Treasurer) under King William Rufus (William II). He acquired the reputation as an astute financier and appears to have played an important part in the compilation of the Doomsday survey. His name is regularly connected with the rapacious extortion and taxation from which all classes and the Church suffered between 1087 and 1100. He personally managed sixteen abbeys or bishoprics and obtained for himself the wealthy bishopric of Durham in 1099. As bishop of Durham, his private life scandalized the local clergy. He had two sons, for whom he purchased benefices before they entered their teens. Scandalous tales are told of the entertainments with which he enlivened his retirement.

2. "When Flambard was Lord Chancellor, they say, all justice slept and money ruled the land…..he was the mightest man in England save the king, and the most feared and hated….." From *Godric,* by Frederick Beuchner, Harper, San Francisco:1980.

BIO

Robert A. Caldwell is a financial advisor and CPA. His writing interests are in the connection between love and spirituality, and with the emotional and psychological aspects of money. When he isn't writing, Robert enjoys cooking, traveling, and the catching of fish.

3rd Place Winner
MY HORSE APPLE TREE AND ME

Betty Jo Loyd Winbush

My family moved to Lee Street in July of 1939. We left Crockett County because my daddy wanted to make a better living for us than share cropping. At first he got a job hauling cotton, then he started selling wood on his own. He razed houses and sold the lumber and bricks, but he also hauled brick for a brick yard.

We were a large family with my father, mother, and five children. I had an older sister who was married, with two children of her own, and two older brothers who were in the CCCS. My youngest brother was not born yet. Our house was a big house and we had our first inside bath — it had a footed bath tub. We didn't have running hot water, but this didn't bother us country folks; it was July and the water we had was warm enough for us.

There were only three houses on the whole block when we moved in. There were also these horse apple trees on the property. One was a male, which didn't have apples on it, and the other a female tree that did. These trees are also known as Osage Orangewood Trees and Hedge Apple Trees. My tree stood about eight feet tall when we moved in but the female appeared to be a little older and its limbs were loaded with the green softball sized apples. Our cow would walk under the male tree's limbs to swat the flies off it.

My brothers played under my tree. They made catapults and would shoot them old horse apples out of 'em, it's a wonder they didn't kill one of us. They also built a tree house in the female tree after they all grew older. It was a boy's club and if a girl came under it they would drop those old nasty gooey horse apples on them. It didn't take but one trip to their clubhouse to learn to stay away.

Daddy had a wood-yard because you couldn't get coal or gas back then. We cut wood for people to use in their fire places, cook stoves, and heaters. Sometimes the wood was piled as high as the house. Sometimes the workers would back those trucks into my tree and knock a piece of the bark off it, but it didn't seem to mind much at all — just kept own growing.

The war started and my brothers left one at a time to serve their country. One was with the National Guard and was the first to leave Jackson with the 117th Infantry Division. He was in one of the first air planes to land at Henderson Field on Guadalcanal Island. The next one was in North Africa and later in Italy. The third went to Germany. We watched our mother's hair turn snow white with worry over those boys. I missed my brothers, but I always had my horse apple tree to help me get through it. I grew and so did my tree.

We always had ice cream suppers when we lived in the country, and we still had them some times on Saturday afternoon at our new house. While there wasn't much sugar then because it was rationed during the war we always managed to have enough for ice tea and mama's tea cakes. One Saturday we had three freezers going and daddy said I'll bet those boys of ours would like some of this ice cream." He got up and got in the old truck and about thirty minutes later came back with about ten soldiers. They were stationed at Union University learning to be airplane pilots. Some of them had never had home made ice cream and didn't mind turning the cranks on those freezers. We would sit under my horse apple tree and talk until dark about their home towns and families. The soldiers would come back to visit and bring their friends. We didn't have ice cream all the time but mama had ice tea and her tea cakes. But when the ice plant just down the street from us found out what we were doing they gave us ice for the soldier boys — for a bowl of ice cream of course.

I was sitting on the porch one day in August of 1945, and here came this soldier up the street. He was home on leave and coming to see his uncle, who worked for my daddy. He didn't know it but he was going to be mine. He was at the Po River with the tenth mountain division when the war ended and was quite a hero. He earned the Silver Star, Bronze Star with two clusters, and in all he had seven medals. My parents would not let me go out but once a week when we were dating, so we spent a lot of hours sitting under my tree.

We married in 1946 and moved into one of the other houses on the block that daddy had bought. We had three children, one girl and two boys, and guess where they played? They built roads under the roots of my tree and drove theirs cars under them; they would get so dirty sometimes we had to wash them off with the water hose before they could come into the house. At one time we had three old tire swings hanging in my tree at the same time. Our daughter said she got her first real kiss from the boy across the street under my tree. I lost my soldier two years ago after his having to put up with me for sixty years, but I still think about all of the good times we spent being watched over by my tree.

Daddy built six houses on the vacant lots around us — four of them had two apartments. My sister moved in next door to us with her four children and the five children she took care of in her day care business. So we always had lots of children playing under the tree. Sometimes we would bring out the old ice cream freezers and sit under it and talk for hours. Whenever the children played hide and go seek it was always home base. We had family reunions, birthdays, and weeney roasts in its shade. Sometimes we would just sit with a cool glass of tea and enjoy the breeze.

Over the years my tree has grown to be twelve feet around at the trunk with limbs reaching a hundred feet across from one side to the other. I have seen five generations of children play under it. They have become doctors, lawyers, college professors, Ph. D's, nurses, policemen and women, state troopers, and just good hard-working people. Some became friends for life, some married each other and had children who played under my tree, and some moved on to other places and things. I have seen my tree covered in ice and snow with its limbs hanging nearly to the ground. It survived many storms, including the big tornado we had here in 2003. My tree may have been bent, but it never broke. Me and my tree have seen a lot together since 1939 and it continues to give me joy. Although the neighborhood has changed with few children to play

under it, there are still the birds and squirrels in its arms for me to watch.

BIO

I am 80 years young. I have lived at the same place for 68 years. My husband and I were married 60 years before he died. We have three children, three grandchildren, and four great grandchildren. I have a daughter with cancer. I grew up with this tree. I look at that tree every day and think of all the things that have happened over the years.

PLAY MISTY FOR ME

Sherry Hughes

HELLO! I AM MISTY AND I AM AN APPALOOSA, AND THIS IS THE STORY OF MY BIRTH. I WAS BORN ON A FARM ONE STORMY NIGHT. MY MOTHER WAS SO LOVELY. SHE IS A SORREL APPALOOSA WITH A WHITE BLANKET ON HER HIPS AND A BLONDE MANE AND TAIL. I ON THE OTHER HAND AM A LITTLE BLONDE BUTTERBALL WITH WHITE SPOTS. I LOOK LIKE SNOW HAS FALLEN ON MY BACKSIDE. MY MOTHER STAYED BY MY SIDE AND LICKED ME UNTIL I WAS WARM AND DRY.

OH, THE HAY IS SO WARM. I DON'T WANT TO GET UP, BUT MOMMY KEPT NUDGING ME WITH HER NOSE. BEING BORN IS HARD WORK. SHE SAID, "COME ON MISTY STAND UP FOR MOMMY. LET ME SEE MY BEAUTIFUL FILLY GIRL."

ONCE I WAS ON MY FEET, I STARTED TO FEEL HUNGRY. MOMMY PUSHED ME TOWARD HER MILK. MMM! SO WARM AND DELICIOUS. MISTY LOOKS AT HER MOM WITH MILK ALL OVER HER FACE.

AFTER MY FIRST MEAL, WE HAD VISITORS. THERE WAS A CUTE LITTLE BOY WITH THEM. HEY, HE IS JUST MY SIZE! HE SAID, "OH MISTY YOU ARE SO BEAUTIFUL. MY NAME IS BLAKE." AT THAT MOMENT, BLAKE WALKED UP TO ME AND PUT HIS TINY HANDS ON MY NOSE. HE KISSED ME ON MY HEAD. I SNIFFED HIM. OH, HE SMELLS GOOD, TOO.

JUST THEN I LOOKED UP. OH MY, IT IS SO BRIGHT OUTSIDE. I WANT TO SEE WHAT IS OUT THERE. MAMA SAID, "MY LITTLE FILLY GIRL, THIS IS CALLED SUN, AND THIS IS YOUR NEW HOME.

I WALKED SLOWLY OUT THE DOOR INTO A BEAUTIFUL PLACE. THE HAY WAS STILL GREEN AND IT WAS STUCK TO THE GROUND LIKE SOFT CARPET ON MY TENDER LITTLE HOOVES.

MAMA WAS LAUGHING AT ME. SHE SAID, " OH BABY THIS IS GRASS." HUH? WHAT DO YOU DO WITH IT MOMMY? YOU EAT IT DARLING. EAT IT? I HAVE YOUR MILK MOMMY AND THIS STUFF IS HARD TO CHEW. THAT IS BECAUSE YOU HAVE NO TEETH. BOY, THERE IS ALOT THAT I HAVE TO LEARN.

FOR NOW MOMMY, I WON'T WORRY ABOUT THAT. I WANT TO GO PLAY WITH MY NEW BOY, BLAKE. MISTY BOUNCES OVER TO BLAKE AND PUTS HER NOSE IN HIS BELLY.

BLAKE LAUGHS AND WRAPS HIS ARMS AROUND MISTY'S NECK. I WANT YOU TO PLAY MISTY, FOR ME.

BIO

My name is Sherry Hughes. I am married to Jimmy and we have 3 boys, Slade, Logan, and Blake. I am a registered nurse at Jackson-Madison County Hospital. I was inspired to write my first book, Rosie's Baby Ali, when my niece was born. I have also written three other books, which I hope to publish someday.

ROSIE'S BABY ALI

Sherry Hughes

HI! I AM ROSIE AND I AM A DACHSHUND. I LIVE IN TENNESSEE WITH MY MOMMY AND DADDY.

MY MOMMY PLAYS WITH ME ALOT, BUT LATELY MOMMY HAS NOT BEEN FEELING WELL. I HAVE ALSO NOTICED THAT HER TUMMY HAS BEEN GETTING REALLY BIG.

I LOVE TO LIE ON MY MOMMY'S TUMMY. IT JUST SEEMS THAT LATELY WE HAVE BEEN GETTING FURTHER APART.

ONE DAY MOM HAD TO GO TO THE HOSPITAL. I WAS REALLY GETTING WORRIED. WHY IS MOMMY SO SICK?

A FEW HOURS LATER, MY MOMMY CAME HOME WITH DADDY. THEY WERE CARRYING A BLANKET. MOMMY SAID COME HERE I HAVE SOMEONE THAT I WANT YOU TO MEET.

SOMEONE? THAT IS AN AWFUL LITTLE SOMEONE. I WENT TO SEE WHAT MOMMY HAD.

IT WAS A BLANKET. ARF! WOW! A PINK AND YELLOW BLANKET THAT HAD BIG BLUE EYES, AND THIS LITTLE SOMEONE STARTED TO CRY. OH NO WHAT DO I DO? PUT SOMETHING IN HER MOUTH.

I GOT CLOSER AND KISSED HER ON HER NOSE. HEY! SHE STOPPED CRYING. I THINK SHE LIKES ME . MOMMY SAID THIS IS YOUR LITTLE SISTER ALI.

I AM NOT SURE WHAT TO DO WITH HER YET, BUT I DO LIKE MAKING HER LAUGH. FOR NOW, THAT WILL BE OKAY. I THINK THAT WE ARE GOING TO BE GREAT FRIENDS.

I JUST HAVE ONE QUESTION. WILL SOMEBODY TELL ME HOW THE PINK AND YELLOW BLANKET MADE MOMMY'S TUMMY GO FLAT?

Walks of Life

Leah Green

On Saturday afternoon April 29, 2006 much to my chagrin, I boarded a plane headed for Phoenix Arizona. My fellow passenger happened to be a nice looking guy who volunteered to put my carry-on bag into one of the overhead bins and offered me a seat. I was so terrified to take off because I had not flown in over six years. He was reading a magazine nonchalantly as I was trying hard not to projectile the remains of my breakfast because I was so nervous about the flight. I looked over at him as I grabbed on for dear life, and politely asked, "So this doesn't bother you?" "No", he politely replied. He informed me that he had flown several times and each time was the same. However, he did mention that one time he made the mistake of eating a McDonald's Big Mac before getting on a plane which made me even more grateful for having sense enough to just drink a smoothie.

When the plane leveled off, I felt like I could at least breathe. So Bryan and I started up a conversation. It turned out that he was originally from Scottsdale, Arizona, and he had transferred to Nashville. I also found out by talking to him that he was planning a wedding with his future bride. He was going to Phoenix to visit her for a few days. I told him that I had recently published a book in which he said "Congratulations". He said that he also had a manuscript that he had been working on for awhile. He also was a songwriter of sorts. An hour had passed by before I asked for the time. He had managed to put me at ease which was no easy feat especially when I heard the pilot say we were going to be traveling at exactly 45,000 feet up in the air.

I decided half way through the flight to look out of the window for awhile. I had forgotten how beautiful the puffy white clouds could be looking down at them. I began to relax as the plane was making its final descent. Then it was time to go to baggage claim and retrieve my luggage. Luckily, I had my Mom along for this trip. At first, we thought that our luggage had been lost as we were waiting for our ride from the airport. We made a sigh of relief when we finally spotted our luggage. We had come to visit my Mom's sister and my favorite aunt.

By Wednesday, we had decided to venture out towards historical downtown where my Aunt Frances has her hair done on a weekly basis. I finally met the infamous Janet who is my aunt's hairdresser. She had heard as much about me as I had heard about her. She was not at all how I had pictured her. Most people rarely look the way that you envision them in your mind. I really did not expect her to have blonde hair although it was probably not her natural color. She was very nice and I really appreciate how kind she has been to my aunt. I love the downtown area there. There is so much history. We went to Lute's Casino for lunch. It is the place where are the movie stars like Marilyn Monroe and Clark Gable used to go for a good time. I bought some souvenirs while I was there at a place called Twigs.

Janet, Mom, Aunt Frances, and I made plans to meet for lunch the next day. We went to this quaint little cafe on the outskirts of town that serves Chinese cuisine. It was really good. I inquired about the Mexican restaurants and Janet told me about the local restaurants. She recommended the green chili enchilada at El Charro's Cafe. It turned out that she was a member of a book club. My Aunt Frances had told her that I had written and published a book so she was anxious to read it and informed me that she was going to tell the book club. I got very excited because my book was now circulating in Arizona.

Perhaps the most interesting part of the entire trip was the journey home. We woke up at about 3:30 AM in order to catch a taxi. The taxi ended up coming early to take us to our next stop which happened to be a Chevron station a few miles up the road. It was hard saying goodbye to Aunt Frances that morning although I was half-awake and half-asleep. We went to this gas station to catch a shuttle that would take us to the Sky Harbor airport in Phoenix. We waited over an hour for that shuttle. During that time, we met one of the workers from the Chevron station. I felt so sorry for that man having to come in to work so early. In the hour that we had been waiting we learned that he was originally from Michigan and his doctor had advised him to move to a warmer climate because of his health condition. He was a widower. He had one son and three grandchildren of which two boys and one girl. They were planning on coming for a visit to see him this summer. He was a very nice man. He even watched out for us.

Along came the shuttle just when we had started to give up on it, and out popped a doe eyed brunette who promptly started loading our luggage into the back of the van and informed us that she was going to get some coffee. There was another passenger who was getting on the shuttle at the Chevron station, a soft-spoken man who was nice enough. He was irritated because the 5:15 AM shuttle was the only one running that day and his flight wasn't until two o'clock. I can't say that I blame him for being irritated. The shuttle driver, Simone was a very entertaining and colorful character. I didn't mind her bubbly personality even though I was trying my hardest to sleep. She and the shotgun passenger struck up a conversation. He was an older man who was headed to Cody, Wyoming. He seemed to know a lot about life and he had a lot of different experiences. He was probably in his late sixties if I had to guess. He was very nice and really seemed to enjoy Simone's company. Simone was a native of Utah and she had grown up as a Mormon. I gathered from the way that she talked she had done a little bit of everything to make ends meet. She even informed us that she was supposed to have gotten married in June, but that she had gotten cold feet.

We picked up some more passengers along the way. They were two girls that seemed to be going back and forth between their parents. They rode in the back of the shuttle. They tried to sleep for a little while and were smart enough to bring a blanket. I had wished that I had brought one because I am so cold-natured. Then when they had woken up, they quizzed each other on Spanish vocabulary.

Did you know that it takes a cactus seventy to one hundred years to grow its first arm? That is a tidbit of information that Simone passed along. Since she had moved to Arizona, she had studied up a lot on legends, colloquialisms, history, and culture. She also made a joke that it looked like the cacti with two arms were making obscene gestures. I had never really thought about that before, but ever since she said that every cactus I saw with two arms, looked as though it were making an obscene gesture.

We finally arrived at the Sky Harbor airport in one piece. My stomach flip-flopped as I realized the countdown had begun for getting on yet another plane. We hadn't managed to get a direct flight to Nashville. We were going to have to make a detour to Texas and then catch a connecting flight into Nashville. We stood in line to tag our luggage and get our boarding passes. There was a little girl in front of me carrying a Beauty and the Beast suitcase. She was so cute despite it looked as though her mother hadn't bothered brushing her hair that morning. She looked back at me and smiled. I thought to myself, this child is not afraid to get on a plane, so why am I?"

The countdown continued as Mom and I grabbed some lunch in the heavily air conditioned airport. Despite, the cold air I was in the mood for a Wendy's frosty. Yum. I thought that it might calm my nerves. Shortly, it was time to board the plane to Houston. The passenger I sat beside this time wasn't in any mood for a candid conversation like Bryan had been a week ago. I was so glad to get off that plane because of the smell of the passenger's tomato juice not to mention the less than smooth landing. It had made me dizzy. Once we landed there wasn't much time until the connecting flight. We were in the "A" group this time so we would get first choice of seats.

I opted for sitting in the middle for the last leg of the trip. Soon we would be arriving in Tennessee. This very nice lady sat next to me on the trip home. She was originally from the Northeast, but she had been living in Houston for quite awhile. It turned out that she and her husband were going to be moving to my hometown soon. She was meeting him in Nashville and they were going to drive west to look at some houses on the market. During the flight, she asked me about restaurants and entertainment. She asked me what I did for a living. I hesitated to tell her that I had published a book and that I just so happened to have a copy in my carry-on bag. My Mom had pulled it out for Randy to look at it. She asked if she could buy that copy and would I please sign it. I was so pleased. It was the smoothest of the flights and it seemed like it took no time at all although it had been a very long day, and coming back we had lost two hours. I turned to my Mom and said, "On this trip especially today, we have seen so many different walks of life". She pondered my observation for a moment, and agreed with me.

On our final descent into the Nashville airport, we looked out the window and there was a cloud cover. It felt like we were walking through the clouds. I looked down at the earth below, and I saw the green trees. The atmosphere is so different here than in Arizona. I felt my ears pop for probably the first time on all four flights. I breathed in the air and it was filled with moisture instead of dry heat. I felt a chill for the first time in a week. And I felt precipitation. Even though it was raining, I was glad to be home in Tennessee.

I am thankful for every new person I met on my trip. I can honestly say that everyone with whom I encountered was genuinely nice, and some even made an impression on me. Each and every person I encountered had a story and some were even willingly to share their stories. Every person had a purpose for going to where he or she was going. People are searching for a place to belong and feel safe. I felt safe in Arizona among family. It was a time that I will never forget. I am a link in a legacy of some pretty remarkable women. I hope that these people who I encountered find or have found that place where they feel safe and belong. We get so caught up in our destinations, that often times, we can't appreciate or enjoy our journeys as they are happening. We live in a very diverse world that is rich in culture. No matter where we travel on life's journey, whether it is Arizona, Tennessee, or any state in between, whether we go for a ride, a flight, or simply pass by someone on the street we will encounter many different walks of life. If it is true that every experience makes us wiser then I learned from pretty valuable lessons on my trip. I learned life is a journey, and on this journey we must learn to overcome and conquer our fears. One of my biggest fears is flying. I also learned that no matter where we go, we are sure to encounter many different walks of life.

Hand Me Downs

Kirby Jones

There are certain things that control a person's life that they have no control over, such was the case in my life. I was the first born child to my mother and father, the first grandchild on both sides of the family, and the first born in a hospital. Therefore, those events took me out of the loop.

What a loop! The hand me down loop.

It started with Ma, my grandmother on my mother's side of the family. She lived in the home place with Uncle Huntington and his family. Back then when I was a small child, it was considered the country but now it's considered part of town.

There was a porch that ran the entire front of the house and had a swing on one end. This meant it was a gathering place after supper or dinner, which ever you want to call it. Most of the time it was supper because we ate in the kitchen, only on special occasions did we eat in the dining room. After super we would go to the swing and Ma would tell stories tha my mother and father would not tell me, which is how I developed my own hand me down and now I am going to hand down to you.

Reelfoot Lake was the only place my family hunted or fished. This day was no exception. My father, Uncle Eason and Uncle Elton, set out to duck hunt on Reelfoot Lake. It was snowing, cold, bitter winds, but duck hunting they did go. After meeting up with the guide they set out to the duck blind. It turned out to be three separate trees.

Reelfoot is known for its cypress trees which stand in the middle of open water.

In three of these trees a board was placed from limb to limb, making a place one hunter could sit. Therefore three hunters, three trees.

The guide placed twelve decoys in front of each tree and left the hunters to the task at hand. The guide would from time to time come back and pick up the fallen ducks which on this day entirely canvasback ducks.

The snow was so thick that you could barely see the lake in the front of you and there they sat three brothers on a board in a tree without anything to protect or heat them from the elements.

Time passes and the guide returns to pick up the three brothers and their ducks. At this time in duck hunting history the federal and state government had joined forces to come up with a limit on ducks, mallards, black duck, pintail teal, canvasback, wood duck, coot, etc… with a total of fourteen ducks. Which brings us to the rest of the story.

Time passes and the guide returns to pick up the three brothers and their limit of ducks. Each of the older two brothers had their limit of ducks. When they got to the tree on which sat the younger brother and picked up his ducks it turned out he had one over the limit. The guide, not wanting to waste the extra duck placed the over the limit duck in the boat and they started towards shore.

As they approached the shore they noticed a man watching them approach. Once on shore they spread the ducks on the ground and began the task of unloading the rest of the equipment from the two Reelfoot Lake boats. The guide calling the man by name and handing him some money asked if he would go to the service station and buy him some gas. He said he had to go back out on the lake and pick up another hunter. The man he had handed the money to was the GAME WARDEN!

BIO

Kirby Jones was born and bred hunting and fishing the Reelfoot Lake. Growing up, no one he knew fished the Tennessee River. Reelfoot Lake taught him many life lessons and has left him with many precious memories from his childhood and his children's childhood. Kirby Jones is a resident of Jackson with a Bachelors degree from Lambuth University and a Masters degree from Memphis State University. He is a retired business instructor who taught at several universities throughout West Tennessee. His wife teaches Spanish at JCM, and they have 2 grown sons.

MY FIRST PERMANENT

Hyla Richardson

Away back in the "good old days" during my junior year in high school, I decided that I must have a "permanent curl" put in my hair. I made the appointment and on that day I entered the establishment with absolute faith in the operator's ability to improve my naturally wavy hair. I believed that I would leave the place with a more becoming style and that I would be made beautiful.

I'm sure the beauty parlor was typical of most small towns of that period. There were shampoo sinks and chairs, manicure tables, dryers, and scattered about the room were tall metal poles from which dangled snakelike wires with metal clamps at their ends.

When I entered I found only one operator and no customers, which meant that I was to have her undivided attention. My hair was longer at that time than I usually wore it and she trimmed some of it after the shampoo. Then chemical pads and metal rollers were used on small sections of hair that was rolled so tightly that it felt as if my hair was being pulled from my scalp.

After my hair was rolled, I was asked to move to a chair under one of the contraptions from which dangled the snakelike cords. The machine had been turned on earlier and was already hot when the clamps were placed on the rollers. The heat activated the chemicals in the pads and started the curling action.

After the last clamp was in place, the operator left me and went to a chair where she had an opened movie magazine and a big red apple. I could hear the crunching of the apple as she ate and read. Soon I began to feel the heat from the machine and the places that were the most sensitive to the heat were at the neck. I sat there and burned while I watched the operator read as she ate the apple. I believed she knew what she was doing. I kept thinking that she would come and relieve my pain and turn the contraption off. Finally she came and said, "You should be done by now."

And indeed, I really did feel well-cooked.

She took the clamps loose and then had me move over to a shampoo sink where she doused water over my hair, and toweled it to remove some of the water. Then she removed the curlers. During that time, I'd had a chance to view myself in the mirror. I was hoping to be transformed into a beauty. However, upon moving over to a chair in front of a mirror where my hair was to be set, I could see at a glance that my hopes were all in vain. My hair had been transformed from a nice brown to a straw-colored mass of wires. I felt horrified at what I saw and I wondered why I had wanted a "permanent". The operator began to try to get the mass untangled with a comb. Tears came to my eyes as she pulled with a comb. At last she had it partly untangled and then she poured on a glue-like substance and began to set my hair in finger waves down part of the way. Next she twisted the rest into small circles and fastened them down with bobby pins. Then she fastened a strong hair net over my head and carefully placed little cuplike covers over my ears to protect them from the heat of the dryer. I wondered if the dryer's heat could possibly be worse than the heat from the clamps. I followed her to a dryer and sat in the chair in front of it. She pushed the dryer down over my head and turned the dryer on. At first the air felt cool, but soon the heat became almost unbearable. I noticed that there were spots that were more sensitive to the heat than others, and I moved my head to try to keep the hot air from hitting those spots with so much force.

After an agonizingly long time, the operator came and raised the dryer and felt my hair. As she moved her hands over my hair, there were little crackling noises. She told me to move back to a chair in front of the mirror. My face was fiery red from the dryer's heat and my eyes had a pained look in them, and they should after all the pain I'd been experiencing. I thought that the rest should be easy and painless. How wrong I was. She removed the bobby pins and began trying to comb through my hair. The hair was stiff from the gooey wave set. As she tried to pull the comb through my hair, tears came to my eyes again. Finally she had it combed to her satisfaction, or maybe she gave up in desperation, and had me step down from the chair.

I paid her and walked out of there thinking that she should have paid me for letting her put me through such torture. I was not proud of the way my hair looked. I hoped it might look better after I had shampooed it myself in a few days. She had instructed me to wait until a week had gone by before shampooing it. I wondered if I could endure it that long.

Every day for a week I avoided mirrors and combed my hair as little as possible. It was torture trying to comb through it, and its horrible burnt color was very obnoxious to me. I rubbed oil through my hair hoping it might help.

A few days after the beauty parlor trip, I found scabs forming on my head and around my neckline. There were places I'd been burned while hooked up to the machine. I learned later that the heat from the machine had caused the chemicals to steam, and that caused the burns.

After treating my hair with steam and different kinds of oils and conditioners, I decided after about four weeks it would never look any better as long as I had that "permanent". I had my hair cut and let it grow back to its natural color and texture.

Later I learned that the normal time for staying hooked up to that machine was about two to four minutes instead of the ten to twelve that I endured.

Needless to say, I never went to that beauty parlor again. Some things in the "Good Old Days" may have been better, but to my way of thinking, my first beauty parlor experience was pure torture.

BIO

I'm a retired teacher and I began teaching in the 40's and taught in varied situations. My majors included Elementary Education, English, Supervision and Administration. After I retired from teaching I helped my son in his photography and video studio. I also taught English to the wives of Arabic students and tutored the students. I write various kinds of writing-poems, essays, etc., some published.

Balance of Chaos

Maggie Elkins

One evening while sitting in traffic, I found my mind drifting, wandering to a myriad of thoughts. With a grimace I turned off the monotone squawk of the afternoon news and realized that I am amazed. I helplessly watch the happenings of this planet that I inhabit and I find myself shaking in awe. Man commits such unspeakable crimes against man and no one seems offended. Life is only worth the jingling change in your pocket. People lie and cheat and steal to have whatever it is they desire...without thought, without pause, without remorse. Within children's minds bloom the seeds of irresponsibility, fear and hostility. Life is no longer simple and golden until graduation from high school. It's a constant struggle with peers, drugs, gangs and guns. The morning at the learning institution is no longer spent worrying if the teacher will ask for answers but if one will make it through the bus ride home. Our civilization is geared and motivated by beauty, money, success and greed. Teenage girls are convinced that bulimia and anorexia will guarantee them friendship and love and adoration. Bingeing and purging is commonplace in order to be the mirror image of the spoiled model on the billboard or movie screen.

And the celluloid circus continues in its never ending monologue of endless million dollar movies that threaten to bore the more intelligent to tears. Hour after hour is wrapped with a garbled quilt of profanity and exploitation. And people spend money to watch? No one seems to care about mankind anymore. Everyone is in a metabolic stupor to speed home and vegetate; no one smiles or waves anymore. Life is one repetitive cycle of work and sleep, without a silent rapture of happiness to be found.

These emotions that I was mired within pulled at my psyche, causing me to sink slowly down into the pit of despair.

I felt as if my world was pulling back from me, recoiling as it will, away from my little vehicle – a mere dot in the sea of mechanical humanity. I floated high, past the electric wires, telephone poles with their hazy streetlights, the carcasses of many a moth within their tombs. Up higher still, away from the smog and soot carried on the breeze, beyond the scope of the birds realm of flight until my world was round and blue and cloud covered...

When my cell phone rang I was pulled crashing back into my car seat like one tossed off a building in a fevered slumber.

"Hello?" I choked, blinked hard against the emotions, sadness and the missing utopia that I lamented for.

"Hi honey...it's mama...I just wanted to tell you that I love you..."

In all our chaos, when the moment seems the blackest and civilization has thrown it's hands up and walked away comes one spectacular word. A word that represents love and truth. A word that restores faith in the world and gives strength when a moment before there was no hope left. And that word is...*mom*...

BIO

Maggie Elkins is a full-time author of short stories, fictional novels and the "occasional" poem. She lives with her husband and their feline, canine and feathered children in Arlington, Tennessee.

For Dee

Maggie Elkins

She was born on June 14, 1920, the fourth of five children. She witnessed the death of her mother when she was only five. She raised herself up from near poverty to attend and graduate from high school. As a teenager, she was lanky, tall and athletic, named All-State basketball player two years in a row. As an adult, she pursued the dream of her heart, graduated from nursing school very high in her class, and started work immediately in one of the prestigious hospitals of the time. Her lineage was festooned with success stories; her older sister worked along side America's Finest rebuilding Pearl Harbor, her only brother a revered sheriff and chief of police. Her own career as a decorated nurse with hands made for healing and caring...

She suffered through her first marriage, the loveless union a centrifuge for her young fears. She had the courage to break free when divorce was uncommon and found the one true love of her lifetime while still in her early 30's.

Regardless of her stellar life, the years forged with adversity. A witness to the death of two of her sisters to a disease with almost no cure, she lifted her head high, pausing only momentarily to grieve the loss and somehow find the spirit to continue forward. Her heart near breaking, she surrounded herself with remaining family, cuddling close, safe and protected. However, life dealt another harsh blow when her husband, the man who loved her to forever and back, lost his life in a tragic motor vehicle accident in September of 1974. How did she keep a part of her heart from dying that day? We may never know. She persevered on, even with the emptiness echoing about her, the cold and empty house, the lonely bed at night, she succeeded to become stronger, wiser, and never forgot her beloved...

In the passing years, she helped raise her spoiled granddaughter and assisted her only child to rise above the bonds of an abusive marriage. She stepped in countless times to hand hold, praise and pat on the back. Her hugs held wisdom, and love and strength and heart. As her nursing career progressed, she helped those younger than she relish their golden years. Yet, with the beginning of her 50th year of nursing, she was diagnosed, struck down by the illusive cancer that had buried her sisters' decades before. Within six months, she was dead. The heart, the soul, the woman that I admired and loved dissipated before my eyes on April 21, 2001.

My grandmother was truly one of the strongest women I have ever known. She departed from my life almost six years now, and it still feels like yesterday that I held her hand and whispered for her not to go. Pleaded, please...just another day, another moment within the bright spotlight of your essence. I can only aspire to be half the woman she was, even if I am offered two lifetimes to live...

Within my mind, I imagine that she is alive and well, doing all the things she always desired to do. She is still beautiful and vibrant and smiling, truly immortal within my heart, residing within my soul. If I close my eyes I can feel her arms around me, a tight embrace, whispered words of love and caring caressing my ear. Even now, as I sit here, I can recall her perfume, the fudge she made at Christmas, the first words she would speak during our Sunday chats and I realize that nothing is trivial. Nothing is ever trivial.

Our mortality cascades about us like darkened cloaks; waiting...watching...until one day it swings to envelop us, only to spirit us away from this life and another to begin. Never miss a moment to hand hold, to hug tightly and whisper those important words now before they're mere memories...arrayed with saddened melancholy smiles...

A Harmonious Discord

Erin Wyatt

Crouched in the frame of a half-open door, a wild-haired girl peered into the street. She grinned, biting her lip for silence as she slipped out, creeping behind a parked truck. Sun glinted cheerily, almost painfully, off the metal. Her hiding spot, maintained in the awkward position of one foot on the tail gate and the other in the air, left her in the worst of the glare to any approaching. Such as the youth sighing down the pavement.

A soft hum came from the boy. Dark hair hung in his eyes, head half-bowed to the mournful melody of his song. But, his gaze jerked to the girl's, meeting her eyes despite the sun. The grin claimed both faces.

With a glance behind him, he leapt forward, landing inches clear of the truck-bed. Their eyes locked, a nod exchanged, and the two vanished inside, swinging the door shut in forced, but maintained, silence.

Inside, the girl giggled helplessly while the boy danced to a new hum, something akin to a circus song.

"Harmony," the boy smiled, "When do you think they'll notice?"

Rolling her eyes light-heartedly, she replied between snickers, "That we're gone? Tomorrow? I'm not sure. They're not too observant, Cat-Cat."

"Never are!" Cat laughed, turning on his heel to face her, hand extended to exclaim, "Dance with me, Harmony!"

A burst of hilarity struck the two, saturating the very air of the messy den. In the midst of their now-music-less dancing, Harmony dodged Cat's booted feet for the fifth time. She humphed at him, eyes alight as she fought by giggles.

"Careful, Kit-Cat!"

Cat, in response, shook his shoes off with a touch of the opposite foot and a rather impressive kick. To that, Harmony shed her sandals with the flourish of landing them atop the broken TV set. The dance continued.

Happy minutes spent themselves with a grin. But, the cheer broke. A knock smacked into the door, stilling the dancing duo, as a voice shrilled, "Harmony!"

The girl in question leaned closer to Cat, whispering, "It's Ms. Clara. What should I do?"

"Pretend to be productive with something?"

Harmony glanced around the room, before lunging to the closet. She dug into the disaster inside. Momentarily, she smiled, then withdrew what was once an intact broom. That sigh was far from pleased.

"Do we have any cleaning stuff that isn't broken?" she queried, dangling the snapped broom stick in front of Cat's nose.

He blinked at her. "We have cleaning stuff?"

That response barely left him time to duck the handle. Opening his eyes cautiously, he watched the girl discover everything from long-dead pens to matchless shoes to still-functioning electronics. Harmony's eyes alit. With a heavy tug, she unearthed a projector, hauling it out of the closet masses, only to plop it on the floor and point it vaguely in the direction of a fairly blank wall. Slowly, it flickered on.

"Harmony?" Cat mouthed.

She turned with a grin, gesturing grandly to the now-lit wall. "We're studying the science of light!"

The grin spread to Cat, "Good excuse- I mean, of course!

The effects of light! How fascinating!"

Again, Clara hit the door, "Harmony!"

"Coming, Ms. Clara." Harmony strode to the door, calmly revealing the annoyed woman, "My apologies. Have you been waiting long?"

"Not long." Clara stood straight, eyes cold on Harmony. "What were you doing?"

"A minor experiment with my brother. On light."

The woman scanned the room, eyes falling briefly on the projector. "Fine but don't be late for my class."

"I wouldn't dare." The door closed, narrowly missing Clara's aristocratic nose. Careless, Harmony turned back to Cat, speaking indifferently of science. Nothing more came from Clara but a faint smirk as she stalked off the doorstep.

When, at last, the duo assured themselves of their solitude, they burst into laughter.

"I can't believe she fell for that!" Cat snickered.

Harmony gasped out, "What'll you do for your dorm mates?"

A fist slammed into the door, shaking it in its frame. Both siblings quieted. Their blue eyes met in realization until Cat grinned.

"Guess we'll find out."

BIO

A Christian teenager, Erin Wyatt currently is in the midst of applying to colleges while trying to finish her senior year at the University School of Jackson. She has been writing fiction and poetry since elementary school, receiving encouragement from many sources, including teachers, friends, and family.

The Meanest Turtle in West Tennessee

A True Story by Larry Workman

It was a beautiful spring day in West Tennessee, just north of the intersection of Interstate 40 and State Highway 412. Larry and Shirley were enjoying the first signs of spring, new green on the trees and a warm sunny morning. The breakfast at Gunther Toodys, a local diner style restaurant with a 1950's theme, was filling. As they were bemoaning the oversize meals they had just consumed, he noticed something in the road ahead.

As their car approached it suddenly became obvious that a turtle was attempting to cross the roadway. In the past ten years since they moved to Tennessee, it has become a familiar sight to see various types of wildlife attempting to cross the road. Sometimes the squirrels give the impression that they can't make up their minds. Should I go right? No, I better go left. No, right! That didn't work! I'll just go straight down the middle of the road, and maybe that car will miss me!

So Larry decided that he would do a wildlife friendly deed, and help the turtle's quest. He pulled over to the shoulder of the county roadway and walked back to where the turtle had already made it about five feet onto the macadam. Although the roadway lacks heavy traffic, the speeds are up in the 50 mile per hour range. So Larry set the hazard flashers to alert others of the action of support taking place.

As Larry walked up to the turtle he noticed its size. This was not the 5 inch diameter, or CD size, version. The shell on this "guy" was 10 to 12 inch. Larry works his way around to the tail end view and prepares to pick it up. He bends down and grasps the edge of the shell between the front and back legs. At the same instant, the legs of the turtle shot out to their full length, and it appeared to arch its back similar to a cat. The head shot out and spun around to a about the half-way point of it shell.

Larry recoiled and jumped back at the reaction he had begun with natures "slow poke". He also realized that the hissing and grunting noise was coming from the turtle. This was the beginning of a nature lesson that Larry was about to get. The vicious look in the eyes of the turtle, and the fact that he was on the attack was a surprise to Larry. This was enough to cause Shirley to look for refuge over by the car, and start laughing at the boogie between Larry and turtle.

This normally docile and shy creature of Mother Nature had suddenly changed. It's actions were no longer stereotypical slow and methodical, but much faster and aggressive. As the turtle was turning around to get a head-on view of the cause of its reaction, Larry was also attempting to keep a position behind it. The turtle and Larry did a few "doe-see-doe's", while Shirley kept her distance and was bent over in laughter at the hullabaloo. Finally Larry was able to make it part way down into the gully which was the beginning of the turtles trek. When Larry reached a point that put him at turtle eye level he looked into those fiery turtle eyes and began begging for an attack. There was Larry with hands chest high, palms up, and curling his fingers in unisons chanting "C'mon you want a piece of me!" to the grunting amphibian.

The coaxing, while still annoying the turtle did nothing to make it move toward safety as Larry had planned. The turtle's thick ugly neck was outstretched with mouth poised for clamping on anything that got close was the only reaction afforded to his molester. Just as determined to move this ungracious recipient of good intentions, Larry came back up to road level for a different method. They made another couple of revolutions as Larry attempted to position himself to the rear of the serpentina.

Finally in the correct position Larry "boots" him toward the gully and away from the roadway centerline. The short quick trip was almost disastrous for the turtle as he was almost overturned, leaving him helpless. This action while relocating the turtle in the correct direction caused more fervor in the shelled creature. Again, he spins around and with fire in its eyes now is on the attack toward its assailant. No longer a "slow poke" he again charges instead of retreating as Larry would have wished.

With its large mouth open just waiting to get within a distance that would allow the strong jaws to clamp on to its enemy the hissing and grunting continue. Literally in hysterical laughter over by the car, Shirley is watching the proceedings. Wondering all the while how in the world does Larry get into these predicaments.

Over in the area of conflict Larry is approaching the shelled one with the sole of his shoe vertical, in a position so that a strike would only hit the flat surface and not expose his toes to any danger. With desperation the assault is made, and there is a wallop to the shoe sole as expected. The force is enough to cause Larry to almost lose his balance, but luckily nothing was clasped in the turtle's jaws.

Once again Larry was able to get the turtle heading toward the gully and quickly got into position to give some more persuading toward turtle safety. This time the idea was accepted! With its head continually looking back over the shell, hissing and grunting all the way the shelled victim finally headed for the security of the tall grass and swampy confines of the gully.

Shirley still in a state of hilarity over the activity between Larry and one of Mother Nature's creatures is still at a safe distance by the car. Finally, feeling successful in saving this turtle from certain demise; Larry makes his way over to his wife and thanks her for her support. They get back into their car and continue home.

Now every time they leave home for work, or going into town, they travel that section of road and Larry is always looking for the meanest turtle in West Tennessee.

BIO

For the past 12 years Larry Workman, and wife Shirley, have been transplanted residents from Southern California. He is a Product Manager for LASCO Fittings, Inc. in Brownsville. This story, of a true experience, and has brought pleasure when retold to their local friends.

Just Another Summer Vacation

Billy Cotner

It was toward the last of July and we had just finished our farm work for the summer. The cotton had been chopped, plowed, and laid by until picking time in September. The fruit jars were filled with the vegetables from the garden and the hay was in the barn for the winter. It was time for my one week vacation before starting the fifth grade at Browns School. I always spent this time between both McNairy and Hardin County visiting my cousins. My cousin Bobby and I had spent many hot summer days riding the back roads on his bicycle since I didn't have a bike of my own I always rode on the handlebars. It was not a bad seat if you could keep your feet out of the spokes; this caused undesirable pain to bare feet. Our favorite place to ride was down Hamburg Hill, not to be confused with Hamburger Hill of World War II fame. This hill was named after the nearby village of Hamber. This was a very long steep hill in which two kids on a bicycle could reach incredible speeds before reaching the bottom. We realized that one little zig that should have been a zag and we would have been hamburger meat on the loose gravel. One the last ride of the day we got a double taste of reality that we will always remember. We were half way down the hill and still gaining speed when we heard the shrill sound of a siren, we both looked back just in time to see a 1946 Ford top the hill at such speed that it left the ground when it crested the hill. "In hot pursuit" was the sheriffs' patrol car; it was completely obliterated in the dust except for the lone red light blinking feebly through the dust.

We were completely helpless on the speeding bicycle. We had nowhere to go and it wouldn't have mattered anyway because when Bobby looked back the front wheel hit loose gravel and we both went sailing. We both plowed long furrows through the loose gravel. Surprisingly we were both still alive although I had a hard time convincing myself. We would both definitely have to grow a lot of new skin.

In the meanwhile the fleeing felon had apparently looked around to see what had happened to us and lost control of his car in the loose gravel and flipped his car twice landing in Uncle Andy's cotton field.

Uncle Andy witnessed the entire spectacle from his front porch and one of the first things that I could remember was him squatted over me with snuff dripping down his chin from both sides of his mouth, picking up my arms and legs as if to see if they were still attached. Uncle Andy walked us home where Aunt Effie cleaned and disinfected us from head to toe, and then wrapped us in torn up bed sheets. We looked like mummies when she was finished with us.

We both slept late the next morning, but we were awakened by the sheriffs' voice on the front porch. He had dropped by to check on our well being. We were straining our ears to hear as Uncle Andy inquired about the man driving the car. "Well I booked him for drunk driving", the sheriff said, "He asked me last night how the boys on the bicycle were". "I told him that I heard that they died". "I was just joking with him but when I went to check on him this morning the crazy sum buck had hung himself".

I was forced to retire from Ormet Aluminum after working twenty three years in the technical department. I did not feel that I was rendered disabled but no one would hire me; therefore I dedicated the rest of my life to mission work. In the past six years I have helped build three chapels in Brazil. I am now serving on the Disaster Relief Team which kept us busy after Hurricane Katrina. I am also serving in the Barnibus Ministries at First Baptist Church. I now have time to spend with my Grandchilden. This is my fifth entry in "The Talent Among Us" and I have been published in two national magazines.

BIO

I was forced to retire from Ormet Aluminum after working twenty three years in the technical department. I did not feel that I was rendered disabled, but no one would hire me; therefore I dedicated the rest of my life to mission work. In the past six years I have helped build three chapels in Brazil. I am now serving on the Disaster Relief Team which kept us busy after Hurricane Katrina. I am also serving in the Barnibus Ministries at First Baptist Church. I now have time to spend with my Grandchilden. This is my fifth entry in "The Talent Among Us" and I have been published in two national magazines.

The Bandit

Shirley Yockem Barker

Reggie was sitting in the tent munching on a juicy apple. He was listening to his brother Logan and his friends telling scary stories. Reggie had a hard time convincing Logan to let him come on the camp out because he was afraid of the dark. Logan was afraid he would embarrass him in front of his friends but finally he said yes.

"Hey, Reggie are you scared yet?" taunted Logan.

Reggie sat up straight, held his head up, and replied, "No! Are you?" Reggie knew he had to be brave no matter how scared he was. The lump in his throat was getting bigger by the minute, and now it was time to turn out the lights.

Reggie lay nestled in his sleeping bag, afraid to close his eyes. It was dark in the tent, and he heard noises coming from somewhere outside. He started to call out to the other boys, but knowing he would be made fun of decided to check things out himself. He crept very quietly to the door of the tent trying not to wake the others. He peered out to see what was making the strange noise he was hearing.

There was something moving in a patch of grass beside the trash can. Reggie crawled out of the tent and stood up. He briefly wondered if it was safe to make a mad dash toward the house. The lights were on so he knew Mom and Dad were still up. He stood frozen in his tracks, silently watching the patch of grass.

With a leap, something landed on top of the trash can, causing the lid to crash to the ground. A ball of fur disappeared into the can. The can rocked back and forth as the creature scampered around inside it. The can turned over, and with a loud noise, crashed to the ground.

Bang!

Reggie saw the little bandit face poke its head out of the can and he realized, "This is just a raccoon, and nothing to be scared of."

The noise had awakened the other boys and they frantically came running from the tent screaming.

"Help"!

"Run, Reggie, run" Logan yelled. "There's a wild animal coming this way"!

"Don't be afraid, Logan, it's just a raccoon after the scraps we threw in the trash can after we ate. I promise I won't let it hurt you."

Looking at the frighten raccoon, and feeling embarrassed Logan said, "Reggie I will never tease you about being scared again. You are very brave. You can go camping with me anytime."

The boys returned to the tent, crawled back into their sleeping bags and relaxed.

As he lay there Reggie noticed the tent wasn't nearly as dark as it had been. He grabbed his flashlight thinking, "I must have unconsciously turned it on," but the flashlight wasn't burning. When Reggie turned to lay his flashlight down, he saw the moon. The beams from the moon were shining in through the window, lighting up the entire tent.

Reggie lay there silently staring at the moon. The glow gave him comfort. He relaxed, and drifted off into a deep and restful sleep.

The next thing he knew, Logan was saying, "Come on Reggie, wake up! Mom has breakfast ready for us. The others have already gone to eat."

As the two brothers walked toward the house Logan said," Reggie you're a real trooper. You didn't scream, or turn you flashlight on a single time last night."

Reggie beamed with joy at his brother's praise.

As they entered the house Reggie silently thanked the little furry bandit. Not for stealing scraps, but for helping him to overcome his fear of the unknown, and for giving him courage.

BIO

I have a diploma in children's education, a Child Development Associate, and a diploma in writing for children and teenagers. I'm a retired pre-school teacher, Sunday school teacher, and church youth director. I've written several non-published children's stories.

Bonnie
A Children's Story by Joyce Corley

Once there was a very nice man and woman who married and were happy for many years. They lived in a small town, and even though they were very happy together, they were lonely.

After a few years they had a little girl and named her Bonnie. This made them very happy and they were not lonely anymore. As Bonnie grew it was time for her to go to school. Bonnie told here mother and father that she wanted to learn to play a musical instrument. This pleased her parents very much. They asked Bonnie what she would like to play, and she said the piano.

Her parents purchased a beautiful baby grand piano and moved furniture around so they could have it in their living room. Bonnie was so excited. She began to practice, but the sounds were so loud and awful that her mother had trouble working, her father could not watch TV, and the cat would run outside. Bonnie became disheartened with the piano and decided she would try the trombone.

Her parents sold the piano and purchased a new trombone, but the root….toot…toot sound was so bad that mother, said "oh my goodness" father said "oh me" and she broke a new vase trying to learn to play. "This just will not work," said Bonnie to her parents. So she decided to play the drums.

Again, her parents sold the trombone and purchased a beautiful new set of drums. Unfortunately the Rum….Bum….Bum…. sound of the drums gave her mother a headache. Her father could not read his paper in peace, the cat went outside, and the dog howled and howled. "This will never do," said mother. "There has to be something she can play." said father. "The drums are just not for me," said Bonnie.

One day there was a big parade in town. Bonnie and her parents were very excited. They attended the parade and when it began they saw a baton majorette in front and leading the parade.

"Oh! Oh!," cried Bonnie with a new excitement, "that is what I want to do!"

Bonnie's parents sold the beautiful set of drums and spoke with the baton teacher at Bonnie's school. Bonnie began to practice every day in the front yard and became quite good at twirling the baton. Mother could do her house work without any problems and no headaches. Father could read his newspaper and watch TV without being interrupted by screeching sounds. The cat could play happily and the dog could play and sleep peacefully.

Soon, the town was planning a big 4th of July parade. The whole town was so happy and worked very hard putting the parade together. The City called Bonnie's baton teacher and asked if she had a student that could lead the parade. The teacher called Bonnie and talked with her mother and father. They were very pleased. They told Bonnie that the City wanted her to be the baton majorette who leads the parade. Bonnie was so excited, she could hardly believe her ears. She worked even harder because she wanted her twirling to be perfect.

At last, the big day arrived for the parade. All of the city officials were there, all of the schools had their bands, and many floats were lined up along the streets. The big red fire engine started its siren and the parade began. Right in front was Bonnie twirling her baton as the band began to play.

Her mother and father were so proud as she passed by they said "that is our daughter." Her teacher was smiling from ear to ear because Bonnie was doing such a fine job.

Everyone cheered as Bonnie lead the parade through town. Afterwards her mother said, "You were wonderful today dear." Her father said, "Everyone had a good time at the parade, because you were such a good leader." The City officials asked Bonnie if she would lead each parade for them.

This made Bonnie very happy. That night when bedtime came she said her prayers and thanked God for allowing her to learn how to twirl, to be able to lead the parade, and for her loving parents who believed in her. That night Bonnie, mother, father and even the dog and cat slept very well.

BIO

Joyce Ann Corley grew up, and resides in Madison County. She attended Beech Bluff School from elementary through high school. Joyce attends West Jackson Baptist Church where she is very active in various organizations and serves on several committees. She is the vice-president of a local bank and Administrative Assistant to the bank's City President. Joyce's hobbies are, "People, reading, cooking, and flowers." Joyce has recently released her first book, "The Elf and the Umbrella," published by Main Street Publishing. The beautifully illustrated book is an adaptation of several classic nursery rhymes from Joyce's childhood.

Three Little Words

Donna King

It was the night before Thanksgiving, 1982, and I was standing by the hospital bed in a state of disbelief. My grandfather, Walker Lay, had suffered a stroke that had left him unable to speak. He had been in the hospital for over a month. Every day after work, I went by the hospital to check on Papa in the hopes that he would be able to talk again. And every day, it was the same. No words would come, no matter how much I could see in his soft blue eyes that he wanted to speak.

I was six years old when we went to live with Papa and Grandmother. My parents had divorced, so my brother, Kirk, and I, along with Mama, moved to their homeplace called Hideaway Acres in the Nixon Community.

It was a wonderful place to grow up. Hatley Creek cut through the pasture to make two wide-open fields to explore. On hot, summer days, the pasture became a race track as Kirk and I rode across the tall grass on Papa's Tennessee walking horse, Sandy, and his old mule, Jence. Kirk, who is older by 17 months, always got to ride Sandy and I was left to ride the mule. Kirk and Sandy always won, but Jence and I gave it all we had!

Papa's huge, two-storied red barn was a magical backdrop for swinging on a dusty rope through the hayloft with our cousins, Tom and Danny Smith. Our days were spent building forts out of hay bales and having corncob battles. Climbing up the corn elevator and jumping over into the crib full of shelled corn was more than just an adventure. It was a rite of passage. Yelling "Geronimo!" as we took the leap with eyes squeezed shut still echoes in my mind. Tarzan, Jane, and Cheetah had nothing on us!

But the best thing of all was getting to be with Papa every day. He was a tall, broad-shouldered giant of a man who worked hard from sunup to sundown. His ready smile, quick wit, and common sense approach to life and living made him a favorite with everyone. He loved to talk and could always tell the most fascinating stories. Sometimes the electricity would go off and the whole family would sit in the dusky twilight listening to Papa tell story after story about anything and everything.

He was a hero in my eyes and quickly became a father figure to me. He never tired of showing off his grandchildren and I basked in the attention he gave me as his only granddaughter. After my open heart surgery in 1959, he always wanted me to show my scar to everyone. "Show 'em your scar, Cissy," he would say, and I would dutifully pull my shirt up for anyone to see. Papa wasn't teaching me to be an exhibitionist. He had sold his horse, Seabiscuit, for $600 dollars to pay for my surgery and I'm sure he was just wanting everyone to see what a good return he had received on his investment!

Papa was proud of me and I knew without a doubt he loved me. There was only one thing that was missing. I don't remember ever hearing him say to me "I love you."

As I stood by his hospital bedside that day, I wanted more than anything to hear those three words. But Papa had not spoken a single word since the stroke and I was afraid I might never hear him say them.

I suddenly realized that I wanted to be sure he knew that *I* loved *him*. I began to stroke his forehead as I leaned over to look in his eyes.

"Papa, I love you," I whispered.

"I love you, too, Cissy," he said, as plainly as I've ever heard him speak.

Papa passed away the next morning.

BIO

Donna King has spent 30 years as an educator in the Hardin County School System. She has been a classroom teacher, elementary principal, and is currently a system-wide supervisor. She enjoys researching and writing family history and lives in the Nixon Community near Hideaway Acres with her husband, Bobby, and their dog, Itsy.

A Ghost Story

d n english

One night around eight o'clock, I had to go up to the office at the Pythian, to pick up some paperwork. The Professor was busy with a research project so I was alone in the car. For some reason, I decided to drive down Sycamore Street (that runs beside Riverside Cemetery). As I turned, appearing out of nowhere, this large black Lab looking dog ran in front of my car! Fortunately, I am not known for driving fast, so it was not hard to stop.

Now, you see I had just finished reading a Navajo mystery involving skin walkers. They are evil ones who can appear as animals, to throw their victim into confusion, so my imagination was running wild. As I caught my breath, I watched as the dog ran toward a man on the ridge in the cemetery. The man appeared to have on a uniform of some kind. Suddenly, the dog and the man just faded away. It was then, I thought I had better go on up to the office.

When I reached the office, I called a friend of mine who was a Civil War Buff. He has also played one of the individuals that was buried in Riverside Cemetery in the Riverside Cemetery Fund Raisers. I told him my story, then he reminded me about the time we had been standing in the Cemetery after the walking tour. We were talking to another gentleman when the three of us saw a solider walking down the hill. "Remember," he said, "we all thought it was another actor but then they told us that I was the only one in a Confederate Uniform." I laughed because I did remember that afternoon and how fast the person that had been with us had left the cemetery.

"Since you brought the subject up, let me tell you what happened to me on Britton Lane Battlefield one night," he said. "It was late one night and I had decided to go out the night before the Encampment we had planned for the weekend." He went on to tell me that he was wearing his Officer's Uniform, had his tent set up and was enjoying his campfire. Rain started to fall gently so he laid down inside his tent. He went on to say, "I must have dozed off because when I woke up, the fire was out and I was still in my Uniform." From the woods he heard voices and footsteps.

79

Thinking it was some of the guys coming out to scare him, he decided to get the drop on them first. He told me he slipped around until he could see three young men in uniform walking toward the tree he was behind. He stepped out, expecting to scare the men but instead one of them walked up to him and said, "Sir we have lost our way and just want to go home." My friend said that after he regained his composure, he realized these men did need directions. "Sons," he told them, "you have served as heros. It is time to go home. You are dismissed."

"d," he said, "as soon as I said it they turned and walked away but they did not walk they faded. I went back to the camp, crawled in the tent and closed my eyes. The next thing I knew, it was morning." My friend took a deep breath and continued, "I walked down the path to the woods and sure enough there were my footprints. I had been in the woods. It was not a dream. So I guess we can say there may be soldiers in several of our battlefields or cemeteries, where unknown soldiers may be still waiting to go home." With that, he hung up. Maybe that is what I saw. Who knows? Where did the dog come from and where did he go?

Poems

1st Place Poetry Co-Winners

1st Place

"Still Waters"

Merideth Allyn

Eyes so full of blue-smoky soul
One could drown in them.
Long, black lashes covering a cream and rose complexion
Might save his hidden still waters from
The curious and admiring.
I don't know.

Always attendant. Back always straight.
Sitting naturally in lotus,
I wonder from what age he hails,
And what he has to offer?

For there is something beautifully luminescent
About him.
Speaking rarely,
One could easily fall into the black hole
Of his innate knowingness.

His age is only eight.
But already he teaches.

1st Place

KID STUFF
Bobby King

This is BIG, this is small.
This is short I, this is tall I.
This is flat,____, this is round, O.
This is up^,this is down v.

*

This is high, this is low,
 *

This is fast, >>>>>>>>>, this is slow > > >.
This is in, (x), this is out ( ) x.
This is smile, :), this is pout : (

This is two xx, this is four, xxxx.
This is less, **, this is more, *****.
This is BUG, this is BEE.
This is you, :>), this is me (<:

BIO

Bobby King grew up in northwest Alabama where most of his stories are set. He is a children's author and has written three books, *Cold Nights and Hot Biscuits, Hot Biscuits: Second Helping,* and *Bullfrogs and Polliwogs - Poems Just for Kids.* His writing is a reflection of his ideas on family, friendship, and his love of nature. He has a B.S. degree in Education from the University of North Alabama. He is retired and enjoys spending time with his best friends, wife Donna, and their dog, Itsy.

"No Saying No"

Merideth Allyn

A happier child you never saw was Liam.
Eyes of sky
And hair of golden curl,
He was simply too hard at two years
To resist.

To say "no" to this child of the Universe
Was impossible.
You said "no," and the mischievous grin appeared.
And, he continued doing the "no" thing anyway.
Ever smiling and sidling with eyes and legs
Oh so slowly toward you
Just to make sure he was in no real danger.
Still grinning.

You had to smile back.
There was just no saying "no".

The golden-haired child was a
Gift from the sea for
The summer honoring the
Woods with his
Terrible twos that were never
Two terrible.

Pure unadulterated Beauty.
Pure raw Nature.
Pure unconditional Love.
Always present, he was simply now.

The first leaves of autumn fell yesterday
And Liam left today.
Back to the sea from whence he came.

And his grandparents,
Who lived in those woods,
Wept in their home's now-noisy silence.

BIO

    Meridith Allyn Wood was born in Washington D.C., attended National Cathedral School For Girls and graduated from Sewanee Military Academy, Sewanee, TN. Her university majors included literature, theatre, and communications. Meredith is married to Larry Wood, has one child, Art, and two grandchildren: Tate, 8 and Liam, 4.

2nd Place
Poetry Co-Winners

2nd Place
Collateral Damage

Myrlen Britt

It's been stated that war is Hell, at least that's what they say.

But the selfish folks who start them aren't the ones that pay.

State of the art killing machines and planes that fill the skies.

Leave behind collateral damage as a result of someone's lies.

Power hungry madmen from every political stripe.

Hide behind their country's flag and patriotic hype.

A poor man's battle; a rich man's war, someone wisely said.

Right or wrong matters little to families who bury their dead.

In the villages of Afghanistan or on a busy Baghdad street.

Life is cheap and death comes quickly moving on silent feet.

It's sad enough when soldiers suffer as bombs rain from the sky.

But sadder still the innocents who have no place to hide.

2nd Place
MY CEDAR CHEST

Marilyn McCollum

IT IS THE CHRISTMAS OF '96,
AND THE WEATHER ASIDE IS A WINTRY MIX.

I WAS GIVEN A CEDAR CHEST TODAY,
TO STORE MY SON'S TREASURES AWAY.

I REFLECT BACK TO THE LAST HOLY SEASON,
AND THE LOVE WE SHARED FOR NO PARTICULAR SEASON.

IF SOMEONE HAD TOLD ME WHAT THIS YEAR I WOULD RECEIVE,
THERE'S NO WAY THAT I COULD BELIEVE.

I LOOKED AT THE CHEST SITTING ON THE FLOOR,
IT LOOKED LIKE A COFFIN, MORE AND MORE.

HOW COULD I PUT HIS THINGS AWAY?
I WANTED HIM WITH ME, HERE TO STAY.

I OPENED THE LID AND IT SMELLED SO FRESH,
THIS WAS A GOOD PLACE FOR HIS THINGS TO REST.

I SAT ON THAT FLOOR AND CRIED AND CRIED,
BECAUSE YOU SEE MY SON HAD DIED.

I STARTED THIS TASK WITH A HEAVY HEART,
I COULDN'T FIND A PLACE TO START.

AS I LAID EACH TREASURE TO REST,
I RECALLED A MEMORY THAT I LOVED THE BEST.
FROM BABY TO TODDLER, TOT TO TEEN,
I MARVELED AT THE SIGHTS THAT HE'D SEEN.

TEDDY BEARS, CAPS, A SACK OF ROCKS,
I LAID HIS THINGS IN THAT CEDAR BOX.

AS I CLOSE THE LID TODAY,
I KNOW THE MEMORIES AREN'T THERE TO STAY.

I CAN OPEN IT AT A MOMENT'S WHIM,
AND BE WITH HIM ALL OVER AGAIN.

THE ROOM IS NEATER, THE MEMORIES STILL IN TACT,
I JUMPED A HURDLE. I WON'T LOOK BACK.

BIO

My son, Jake, was killed in 1996 in a car accident. That was a year of many "1st's" for me. The first Christmas without him was horrible. My husband gave me a beautiful cedar chest and as I began to fill it, I wrote this poem. I stuck the poem in the chest along with his things and didn't open it again for a long time. Maybe it will give some comfort to others who are going through their firsts without their child. Thank you.

2nd Place
Nature Reigns @ 2003
Myrtle D. Russell

Couldn't print the paper, couldn't run the mail
Tornado touched down. Rain, wind, baseball size hail
People dead, homeless, left in the dark
What is this force that leaves animals frantic, people panicked
Wherever it strikes, leaves unforgettable marks?

Touched down on Sunday, hop-scotched across several states
Hit town close to midnight, thank God it was late.
In the heart of the Bible belt as the Sabbath Day ended
In "tornado alley" where the wind's seldom friendly,
What is this force that hits the same place twice
Can someone explain it, is this some lesson on how to be nice?

Families searching for answers, wanting to make some kind of sense
Of these strange happenings, this chain of events
Events that make men weep, make women stand guard;
Teenagers volunteer for hard labor; and dogs cry in the dark

Rubble piled high, so many pieces of dreams
Oh what unbelievable, heartbreaking scenes
Scraps from churches, homes, businesses, schools
Priceless papers, tangled wires, splintered wood, building tools
Phones ringing off the hook, phones with nary a sound
Emergency crews working overtime, restoring power to the town.
What is this force that makes us change our routine
Makes us forget the barriers and seek the serene?

Super cells triggering mile-long twisters
Moving like jets through the clouds, no eyes, no towers
Nothing to interfere with its power
Children left with questions, adults without answers
Many empty of thoughts, things, hope for the future.
What causes these unstable conditions over which we have no control
When hot air meets cold air and nature's havoc unfolds?
It's the Lord's work and God don't make no mistakes;

It's a freak act of nature like floods and earthquakes;'
It's payback for all the evil we've done to others;'
It's a balancing act; negative karma;
Now don't you go questioning God, you were raised better than that
His will is done and that's a natural fact.
Nature's tough at times, everything happens for a reason
In all things there's a time, in all things a season.

I ponder the question, my wandering mind
Global warming, the ozone layer, poisonous gases, pollution
Cutting down trees, killing birds and bees
And when's the last time you saw a butterfly?
Could we possibly be causing the earth to warm-up, the loud thunder,
This mysterious plunder?

We all have theories, our own beliefs
But on this one thing I think we'll agree
When disaster strikes we seek a higher power
There's a genuine outpour of love, if only for a few hours
We feel it, express it, putting barriers aside
And in "God We Trust" as our spirits rise
We connect with the universe, we look to the wise.
As our souls greet one another and never in disguise.

The force of the wind in the spring brings love.

BIO

Myrtle Russell is co-author of small change: A 28 day guide to eating, thinking and feeling healthier, and enjoys self-expression through poetry. She is health editor for the West Tennessee Examiner News and Classifieds and writes a "Small Change on Health" article for the publication that prints 6,000 newspapers weekly. She is also a past member of the Griot Collective, Inc.

3rd Place Poetry Co-Winners

3rd Place
The Minister's Wife
Poems by Robert A. Caldwell

11/24/2000

The minister's wife dreams
Not of souls saved
but of spring days
Not of lessons taught
but of love lost
Not of ice cream socials
but of wine long forbidden
Not of King James
but of King David
David with Bathsheba
Not of submission
but of sublimation
of the senses
of pleasures
of the flesh
Not of the pious man who
averts
holy eyes
from her bare flesh
but of one
whose gaze devours
her
as a flame
Not of hymns of the faith
but of him
him whose fingers
played her breasts
like harp strings
Not of fire from heaven
but of one

whose touch
created heavenly fire
in her thighs
the minister's wife dreams

11/25/2000

The minister's wife
answered the door
and I saw beneath
the denim
the soft mounds
of her breasts untethered
and wide spaced
and I wondered
if they ached for strong hands
to enjoy them
but for her
strong hands were never
never
at home

11/25/2000

The minister's wife
has two children
but never a lover
to play her lush
body as
Loren Hollander plays
the piano
caressing
with steel fingers
of exquisite gentleness
causing her to rise and
fall with the ripples of a melody
writ on her flesh

11/25/2000

The minister's wife
sits in church and
sweats for
the air conditioning
has failed
and dreams of a man
who would lick the
sweat
from between
her fine breasts and love
love
love the doing
 of it
whose fingertips
would anchor her
slick armpits
as thumbs
rolled
rolled
rolled her nipples
and she
she
she
ground
herself against
his bare
knee but this
she knows to seek not
in the parsonage
washed daily by
her tears

11/26/2000

The minister's wife sits
as the visiting missionary
drones on and
she
wishes for the missionary
position
or any position to
ride
and be
ridden
in the
ancient rhythm
the mounted dance

11/26/2000

The minister's wife walks
alone in the
silent house to
the bedroom and
unlocks
the chest in
the back of her closet
to lift up
the wicked forbidden
silks the gossamer
things she
wears in secret
to lift them out
to inhale her
scent her
cassolett as
would a lover
do

11/29/2000

The minister's wife sits
in the sun
and lets it
caress
her bare breasts
but it
does not warn
her heart
her solar
 lover streaming
through the window
shows more care
than the preacher-man
so sigh she will
for Sol Invictus
and spread her
damp curls for him

12/01/2000

The minister's wife sits
and surveys the congregation
silent seeking
those who care so
little for
sermon and preacher
as she
see there be one
with eyes that pass
over her
as a tongue

12/05/2000

The minister's wife sits
In the cold church
And despairs of the
cold touch
of her sanctified husband
who prefers to embrace
church committees
instead of the warm breasts of his wife

12/05/2000

The minister's wife sits
in despair
over the holy man
who finds excitement
in
alter calls
but not
in
her
ripe body

12/07/2000

The minister's wife sits
in blue silk
pajamas
and
lets butter soft
fabric
caress her breasts
with a shrug
for
the hands of her
holy husband
caress her not

12/12/2000

The minister's wife sat
in her living room
dressed in white
cotton
against summer's heat
white cotton as cloud
cover over
a verdant
landscape
full arms as ridges
peaking breasts as hills
mown armpits as vales
gently rounded plain of belly
dark, tangled triangle
of ancient mystery
of Eve
Pointing
Pointing
Pointing
to a jungle of spices
sturdy legs
willing to part
but not summoned
by her husband O
self seen holy man he
so dream lovers
sought she
Lovers to taste the hills' peaks
Lovers to explore the jungle
Lovers to penetrate deep darkness
Lovers to dream

3rd Place
Grandmartha's Overnight Visitor

Martha McNatt

At dawn
You stir and twine small hands into my hair.
I turn
And with a squeak your toy raccoon
protests my shoulder's weight.
I move and with a push, dislodge the book
That took us both to slumber's gate.

You sit upright with sleepy eyes and tousled hair
and smile at seeing Grandmartha there,
and say Good Morning.
The morn is good, my child so dear
When I awake and find you here.

Alas, so soon sweet innocence with flee,
And smash the bond between you and me.
Hold back, oh time
Let me enjoy
A few more nights with my darling
 Four year old boy.

BIO

Martha is a retired local educator, author of Feeding The Flock, Grandmother's Face In The Mirror, and many articles. She was the poetry winner for Main Street's Talent Among Us II. Martha is also a Library volunteer and author of First Christian Church History.

3rd Place
COUNTRY RAISIN'

COUSIN TUNY

I GREW UP ON COUNTRY RAISIN'
GOT DE-WORMED TWICE A YEAR
TOOK TURPENTINE ON SUGAR
TO KEEP MY HEALTH IN GEAR

GOT CASTOR OIL AND CHILL TONIC
IN THE SPRING AND IN THE FALL
KEPT ME FROM BEING BILIOUS
AND, COUSIN, THAT AIN'T ALL

I LEARNED TO RESPECT MY FELLOW MAN
AND HELP HIM ON THE WAY
MY MAMA TAUGHT ME LOVE AND KINDNESS
TO DO GOOD EVERY DAY

I WENT TO CHURCH ON SUNDAY
SAID MY PRAYERS EVERY NIGHT
CLEANED MY PLATE AND SMILED A LOT
CAUSE IT MADE ME FEEL SO RIGHT

I'M PROUD OF MY COUNTRY RAISIN'
IT TAUGHT ME HOW TO LIVE
THE VALUES OF GOOD LIVIN'
SO MUCH HAPPINESS TO GIVE

SO, CUZ, I STAND BEFORE YOU
A THANKFUL COUNTRY GIRL
CAUSE I GREW UP ON COUNTRY RAISIN'
THE BEST IN ALL THE WORLD!
YESSIRREEBOBOLINKO!

BIO

A Native Jacksonian, 4 children, 4 grandsons, 3 great-grandchildren. Her career spans a lifetime in Radio, Television, Mall Management, Healthcare, Marketing/Public Relations, Co-Author of two books, "CUZ" and "TUNYISMS, ETC", Musician, Speaker, Songwriter, Poet, Entertainer, and has Co-Hosted 70 plus telethons with a lifetime love and advocate for children. She's an energized "MEDICARE MAMA" and EVERYBODY'S CUZ"

FALLOWED GROUND
Gary Kirk

Once she was loved
she would know it,

as the life that was,
the promise that would be,
the story she could tell
to be

who she is now,
more than a memory
embodied in a history
of love's unpromised word.

She knows
she could have given hers.

She waited on the fallowed fields to green.
May was warming up to June,
and the clematis and the honeysuckle
were trying to find their way over the fence
to begin to smell sweet.
And as always she dreamed.

Forever all alone she sowed in her own
dormant seeds of perennial wishes
but they never could compete,
with the summer's wild rose
and the fragrance of her unfulfilled needs.

Silent as silt
she buried herself in the earth.
Creating a memory
that upon her return will be
remembered.

BIO

I am 55 years old, residing in Leapwood in McNairy County by way of Mishawka, Indiana. My family is from here so my heart has been here. I enjoy readin', writin', but not 'rithmetic. So once in awhile I attach words to feelings rather than figuring out the answers.

Goofy Words

Bobby King

Flubdubbery is a goofy word.
Degoop is one I've never heard.
Spell wibblescritch if you choose,
but the goofiest of all is goozywooz.

Bonkerbash sure makes me smile.
Just say kebabble for a while.
Schplittenslod is hard to say,
To spell hexmangulate takes all day.

Have you ever heard the zeebie word,
or learned to say boosicleferb?
I sure can't spell makwirtsenberg,
bejeckle, spoink, or cheedleblurb.
So I'll just forget these goofy words!!!

LET WATERS FLOW @2007
Myrtle D. Russell

Let waters flow to weak limbs and thirsty bodies;
Replenishing sweat and tears lost to summer's deadly heat.
Quenching Waters!

Let waters flow to mouths of innocent, anxious children
Hands outstretched hands, lips smacking; Yearning for sugary refreshments.
Cleansing Waters!

Let waters flow to aching joints, squeaky knees, tired muscles,
To parched lips, scaly skin, and splitting fingernails.
Replenishing Waters!

Let waters flow to barren fields of farmers with empty coffers;
Powerless to produce crops to feed hungry consumers.
Nourishing Waters!

Let waters flow to fish in streams, rivers, lakes;
Uncontaminated; pure; devoid of man's filth.
Natural Waters!

Let waters flow to pregnant mothers carrying unborn embryos;
Waiting in sacs of water for their birth dates.
Nurturing Waters!

Let waters flow to flowers with hung down heads; Forsaken their right to beautify the world;
Drying, dying, returning to seeds from whence they came.
Sprinkling Waters!

Let waters flow mercifully, harmoniously, absent of force
To fragmented minds that fear the wind and rain when they combine forces in madness.
Still Waters!

Let waters flow to thousands trekking miles for a drink;
Never taking the formless liquid or its miraculous qualities for granted.
Sacred Waters!

Let waters flow to wildfires; flames leaping like fire-breathing dragons;
Spitting blazes at weary firefighters praying for relief.
Cooling waters!

Let waters flow to egotistical psyches of world leaders;
Driven by power and greed; Lacking love and compassion.
Healing Waters!

Waste not. Want not.

MARRIAGE

Joyce Billingsby

We sat beneath the sprawling tree
Leaning against each other,
Watching little children run and play;
Where once our parents sat and smiled
To hear our childish laughter —
It seems as though it were only yesterday.

Through the years we laughed and cried,
Fought friend and foe and brother;
Stood toe to toe against the world,
And often fought each other.

We gave and took and compromised
But would not have another;
For what is marriage all about–
But leaning upon each other!

Memory Games

Martha McNatt

I played Hide and Seek with my memories today.
Through half closed eyes I watched them hide in unexpected places.
Some are tucked away among my treasures.
Others are clearly visible,
Awaiting the awakening of my senses.

I observed:

Jessie's lace trimmed hankie folded between the pages of her Bible.
My young father standing beside his favorite mule, smiling at me from a faded snapshot,
A neatly folded olive drab soldier's cap scented heavily with cedar.

In my kitchen, a copy of my grandmother's blue stone salt crock,
A tiny wooden table crafted by my grandfather for his first grandchild,
White linen napkins, dinner accessories for more than fifty years,
Frosted green glasses each one a prize from a box of oatmeal.

Ninety eight, ninety nine, one hundred
"All of you come home free" I shouted.
And home they remain, but free of me they will never be,
For these are memories are mine and I am the winner of the game.

What If ???

Bobby King

If I eat a bag of popcorn will I pop?
If I eat a roasted hot dog
will it make me run and bark?
Will a slice of watermelon
make me wet from head to toe?
Will a crunchy cherry snow cone
make icicles on my nose?

If I eat a bowl of Jello
will I jiggle when I walk?
And will some Snickers candy
make me giggle when I talk?
Will a bowl of chocolate ice cream
make me shiver through and through?
Will blueberries on my cereal
make my little toes turn blue?
                    Oooooo!!!

A Friend is...

Bobby King

... someone who lets you
have the last orange Push Up.
... someone you can eat lunch with
without being invited.
... someone who helps you
pick out a name for your
new puppy.
... someone who helps you
keep a secret.
... someone who always
lets you sit by the window.
... someone who lets
you pick out the movie.
... someone you can
spend the night with and
your mom won't be worried.
... someone you can share
your feelings with.
... someone who loves
you no matter what happens.

(I Got) A Taste of Heaven

Mark Kendrick

I never cease to be amazed
At the power of His love
While walking right beside Him
A sinner cleansed by His pure blood.

The blessings that he sends my way
I never know just where or when
One day a troubled angel
Asked for a prayer, and then …

I got a taste of Heaven
Through a warm and sweet embrace
I felt the depth of my God's grace
As the angel shared her soul without decision.
And while the tears streamed down her face
In my prayer I knew the place
Where she'd be covered always under His provision.
I got a taste of Heaven.

My witness is but one small grain
In the mighty ocean's sands
But how the blessings overflowed when
God's angel took my hand.

My soul can hardly bear to wait
Until the Lord returns again
And when he does I'll tell Him
"I remember that day when …"

I got a taste of Heaven
Through a warm and sweet embrace
I felt the depth of my God's grace
As the angel shared her soul without decision.
And while the tears streamed down her face

In my prayer I knew the place
Where she'd be covered always under His provision.
I got a taste of Heaven.

© 2005-2007 Mark Kendrick

BIO

Past TAU winner. TOWA award winner (writing/photography). Poster art winner (Shannon Street Blues Festival/King Biscuit Blues Festival). Original art/prints found in several U.S. States and several countries abroad. Married to Dale (Wateridge). One son, Caleb. Lifelong resident of Brownsville, TN.

Teacakes and Soda Water

Kimberly S. Morris

One morning I looked over my shoulder and saw yesterday
She winked, blew me sweet-kissed memories
Landing on my right cheek; they tilted time,
She whispered, time heard and I remembered...
Having teacakes from the oven and soda water from the icebox.

A short dumpling of a woman she raised me from her rocking chair
Pieces of my childhood were sewn as the triangles she quilted
Often, little seasoned hands prepared crusts for sweet potato pies
After school, Baltimore Street found me on her porch
She rocked, i swung, the breeze listened.

As i look over my shoulder Dupree Street finds me shelling peas
Not too happy about the purple stained fingertips they leave me
But, she opens her coin purse; gives me 75 cents to go to Bill's Pharmacy
i bought a blow pop, cheese curls and an RC,
While tasting teacakes from the oven and soda water from the icebox.

As i look over my shoulder Pavilion 51 is the best picnic spot at Muse Park
She walked, i followed, we sat – on a bench near the outer banks of the pond,
She reached, i watched, they came quacking and waddling
Taking alms from her palms; she watched, i trembled, they ate;
i felt the duck's bill graze my hand and it didn't even hurt – just tickled.

As I look over my shoulder I see a bus topping the hill of Main Street
She rode, i ran, we walked to the house,
Evening carried us up and down the isles of Liberty's grocery store
She got paid; i was happy; we were rich!
i know, 'cause this time, she bought me a Hershey Bar.

Looking over my shoulder Woolworth's was downtown Jackson to me
Drinks at the fountain, bargains in the bends

She shopped, i sat, we waited till time gave out; money ran out
Yet, we loved one another just the same.

As I look over my shoulder, I see Lake Graham being born
i looked, she marveled, we moved
Along the hollowed ground found as a bed of rocks resting,
She gave me my first taste of Madison County,
Munching on teacakes from the oven and soda water from the icebox.

BIO

I am an emerging writer from Jackson, Tennessee. By profession I am a Social Work Consultant for Middle Tennessee State University. I am also a member of the Griot Collective of West Tennessee. In my spare time I enjoy reading and writing poetry while sipping coffee sprinkled with conversation.

Nectar of Jazz

Kimberly S. Morris

And the beat goes on…

Conversations of love in the key of G
As sound swallows silence in whole pieces
Tickling the anchor of my soul
Notes falling high, reaching low
Landing amidst the inner me
Soulful cries reside with ease
In a forever so smooth I had to move to the groove

And still the beat goes on…

Tasting like the sound of piece
Giving way to the smell of a sweet release
I tried to resist but the note did insist
That I sip the nectar of his melodic juice
Couldn't wage war so I called it a truce
Surrendering as musical waterfalls flowed upstream
My ears saw sound and soul greet the beat

In the sky of its own sunset refusing to stand still
Notes and sounds rising and falling at will
Precipitation falling in a cotton candy sky
Images tiptoeing beyond while words pass me by
Driving down Highland Avenue
Wearing the groove like a pair of old shoes
As the breeze combs my hair with night air

Cause, the beat goes on…

"The Storm"

JAEL

"Its' a mystery why centuries of history are so easily permitted to perish/ centuries of family and loved ones you cherished."/While the rest of us are comfortable; the rest of us are miserable/such an imbalance, but who will rise to the Challenge?

"It's not surprisin'...there's a Storm on the horizon."

"Folks up at night-all late hours- sucking down sleeping pills/ trying to find the power to cure their many ills.

$2200 to restore your life while you're outside living in your car; others seem to live without a mar..it's so bizarre"/" I want to leave", she laments, "but not on my watch; I'm the next generation to be in that March."

"It's not surprising'...there's a Storm on the horizon."

"A man's collecting empty cans to take his wife away; collecting cans late at night and to his wife's dismay…he gets shot that day"

"A man sitting at a traffic light takes a breath, a young girl -18 years old- …walks up and shoots him to death."

There are storms of violence/storms of divorce/storms of bankruptcy/ storms of force.

"It's not surprisin'...there's a Storm on the horizon.

I sense that the Storm is near; Wait! Look! The Storm is here."

117

I AM

L.B. Sloane

I am your brother
I am your sister
I am your mother
I am your father

I am screaming do you not hear me?
I am crying do you not see me?
I am your neighbor do you not feel me?

I hear the roar of inadequacy
The storm of iniquity
The rage of hypocrisy
Where are the ones of responsibility?

I am your brother
I am your sister
I am your mother
I am your father

Lying broken on the ground
Waters rising all around
Levees breaking, hearts aching
I am crying do you not see me?
I am screaming do you not hear me?

I am your brother
I am your sister
I am your mother
I am your father

BIO

L. B. Sloane is part of a team of writers. They have published music and short stories. They love the joy of words.

Suzanne

JAEL

A friend of mine died today
In a way that we're unaccustomed to
She volunteered to let the world take away
The only life she knew

It's so hard to understand
Cause we knew you had a plan
And then you turned and ran-Suzanne

She gave so easily
A soul of generosity
But she could only see
The world's hypocrisy
Such a tragedy

It's so hard to understand
Cause we knew you had a plan
And then you turned and ran-Suzanne

I heard you agonize
And yet refuse to compromise
Always true to yourself
Searching for the good
and yet never understood
And then you said farewell

Everywhere we go – we think
we see your face
but its just a reminder
of what is now an empty place

The words you would impart
Revealed within your heart

Your crying need for love-
But love is like the sky
It's never up too high
For you it was just above

It's so hard to understand
Cause we knew you had a plan
And then you turned and ran-Suzanne

Sometimes we just can't win/but we can't give in/The going will get rough/but we can't give up, Suzanne, Suzanne   (Dedicated to the memory of Suzanne Valentine)

BIO

JAEL was born upstate New York and currently resides in Jackson, Tennessee. He prefers to write under "JAEL" - a family name. He is a songwriter and his songs have been published on the Mercury and Warner Brothers labels. He has also written a short story "There Was a Time…" that has been published by Main Street Publishing. He has also written a published novel and now this poem."

If Life Were Easy

By Beverley Kay Matlock
July 15, 2006

If life were easy, it would be no life at all.
We would never have the chance to fall
From the towers we build so high in the sky,
From all the mountains God built so high.
If life were easy, we would all drive a Cadillac,
Forever sip lemonades on the porch out back,
Could go there in a hundred years,
And, have it all when the dust clears.
One thing is for sure for His Righteous way,
God's love makes for the happiest day.

In A Child's Eyes

By Beverley Kay Matlock
12/06/06

"There's a story in a child's eyes,
It matters not their size.

They are innocent in ways untold.
And they live life so bold.

Those eyes just keep saying love,
And ask blessings from above.

So, hold your arms opened wide,
To the precious child so starry-eyed.

BIO

Life with Jehovah God has made my life worth living because I live Him. This is reflected in my poetry. Without God, I can do nothing. May your days be filled with serving God and our Lord and Savior, Jesus Christ. The Holy Spirit will be your Helper.

Amen

"Great-grandmother"

Sarah Elizabeth Taylor Haney
February 19, 1855 – January 12, 1897
Scotts Hill, Henderson County, Tennessee

I hold an old, worn portrait in my hands.
Her eyes look straight into mine.
Her lips do not smile.
Her long hair is pulled back in a bun.

I wonder what it was like to be my great-grandmother.
Do I see my own blue eyes in hers?
My granddaddy said I have her auburn hair.

She was born in 1855, married at age twenty-one,
Birthed her first child when she was twenty-two,
Buried him when he was nine,
Died in childbirth at age forty-one with her tenth child.
Her eight little children gathered around her bed.

Did she love life or was life too hard to love?
Did she ever dance, sing a song, or visit with a friend?
If I could travel back in time, what would we do?
I would love to brush her hair, see if her eyes are blue, and make her smile.

Katherine Haney Williams
Born September 28, 1950
Jackson, Madison County, Tennessee
"Great-grandmother" written July 7, 2006

"Morning Prayers"

Katherine Haney Williams

I wake early when the house is silent
…before the clock alarms,
…before the TV blares the morning news,
…before the traffic breaks the silence,
…before the dog barks at intrusive critters.

I hear the gentle snore of my husband
And see his outline in the dim light before dawn.
I slide my foot over to touch his foot
Just to be connected without waking him.
I pray for his health and happiness.

I tiptoe to my sons' rooms where they sleep peacefully.
I gently touch their cheeks and hands
And say a silent prayer for long and happy lives.
This has been my ritual for twenty-one years.
They are now young men – college students.

My body has gotten cold in the winter chill,
So I slip back into bed beside my sleeping husband.
He pulls my cold body next to his strong, warm body.
This is heaven on earth; my family is safe and peaceful.
Dear God, I thank you. Amen.

"Morning Prayers" written for Butch, Blake, and Spencer
Valentine's Day 2007
Jackson, Tennessee

BIO

Katherine Haney Williams has celebrated twenty-three years of marriage with Butch Williams. They live in Jackson with their sons, Blake and Spencer, who are students at Union University.

Kathy is the Human Resources Administrator with thirty-three years of service at Pinnacle Foods Group Inc. She researches family history, writes South Side High School alumni newsletters, and writes poetry.

Beautiful Mosaic
Leah Green

The Potter at His wheel
Molding me, Making me

His purpose to fulfill
After His own will

My heart He engraves
My soul he saves

My Spirit He sets free
My Savior is He

The world says His Word is archaic
I know His truth will never diminish

My Utmost for His Highest
I cannot deny
Until I meet Him in the sky

He commands that I say it
The Potter at His wheel

Molding me, Making me
Into His own image

His masterpiece
His beautiful mosaic.

BIO

I enjoy writing works of fiction and poetry. The poem I am submitting is called Beautiful Mosaic. It is a reflection of how I strive to view myself through God's eyes. After all, I am a work in progress. I appreciate opportunities such as these to grow as a writer.

A Garden and a Woman

Frankie Woody

A garden is so like a woman. It is beautiful when it is blooming and growing. The butterflies dance, joyfully, among the colorful blooms, in a garden. It is such a lovely sight to see. But, then the blooms fade with summer and age with winter; and that beauty is hidden from the human eye.

As a woman ages, her beauty fades, in much the same way, a garden's beauty fades. She is no longer blooming and growing, or glowing. Her wrinkles remind us of the gray growth, that we see in the wintertime. In the garden, that decrepid, wrinkled look fades away, with the true beauty of spring. Spring is ushered in so elegantly. It is once again, beautiful to the human eye. Indeed, a garden and a woman share similarities, in the face of time.

Written on one August day in 2006

BIO

Frankie Woody is a farmer's wife and the Mother of one daughter. Frankie has been writing, since she was a child. She remembers writing poems, for her family, at Christmastime. Frankie is a graduate of Murray State University, Murray, Kentucky. She majored in communications and minored in journalism. She received her B.S. degree in 1980.

WEEPING WISTERIA

Frankie Woody

Have you ever thought of a wisteria blossom as a large, purple teardrop? It starts out big and, as it flows, the petals get smaller. Just imagine a great, big teardrop falling, ever so slowly. As they fall, the tears can represent genuine joy from the depths of a soul, or heart-wrenching pain from the past or present, or grief that has been hidden; or release from a burden that has finally been lifted.

The teardrop reminds me so much of the wisteria blossom. The lighter shades of lavender could represent the light that God shines in your soul, or the multi-shades of purple could represent the different degrees of happiness, or the darkest color of purple, on the petal, could represent the darkest days of your life. The shades of purple in the wisteria wind their blooms and vines around an arbor, a house, a tree; the same way emotions can wind themselves around a mind, a heart, or a soul... Some tears are light. Some are frivolous. Some are happy. Some are heart-wrenching. Some tears are hopeless. Some are merely sad. All teardrops are different; just as all shades of purple, are different in the wisteria blossom.

(Inspired by a wisteria vine on The Wildflower Farm)
April 12, 2005

The Horse Apple Tree

Dr. Danny O. Winbush

Osage orangewood tree,
tall and wide, your trunk
and limbs have witnessed
much over the years.

Your limbs have provided much
appreciated cover for lawn chairs,
ice cream mixers, hot summer days,
humid nights, and the occasional stolen kiss.

A place to build complex road systems
for the boys cars and trucks and for
girls to play with their dolls amongst
the roots at the base of your trunk.

You have been subjected to Tarzan yells,
held children upside down from your limbs,
supported tire swings, been used as a catapult
for horse apples, and the keeper of home base.

You watched over us as we discussed
family matters, friends and neighbors,
religion and politics, personal crises, loves lost,
and loves gained without passing judgement.

The keeper of my memories past and
the facilitator of my dreams and wishes to come,
some were lost and some were realized,
but many more were revised along the way.

Thank you Osage tree.
You have been a good friend and
a symbol of strength and tenacity.
And you never revealed our secrets.

The Shadow

Sheila Love Nicholson

I gave Keata away today
I didn't have the words to say
I looked Jason straight in the eyes
This baby girl will always be mine
I gave Keata away today
Her Dad passed away
He is the shadow
That is beside her now
I am the Mom
Going on somehow
The smile on her face
The love in his eyes
Who gives the bride away?
I said I do
It should have been Dad's place
Dad is the shadow
That stands beside her
Her heart stirs
The wedding takes place…

BIO

I have written all of my life. It is something that comes to you and you must write it down to free your soul. I am the mother of four daughters. I am 53 and had my first book (filled with 100 poems) published by Main Street Publishing in 2004. It was my dream. I co-owned a Dairy Queen for 25 years and continued to write.

Two Apples

Thomas Aud

Simple little works of art,
Girt with even
Thinner girdles than
The cheap, painted ones.

Sensuous to the touch
And taste, stirring
The passions of buds
Made to be aroused.

Tiny outlets of emotion
Of the one to the other,
Neither knowing which,
But not feeling the least bit queer.

The one smile warmly
And moves closer,
Causing a candy-red
Never fading away.

They are next to each
Now, still unsure,
Touching, feeling, finding
Copulation impossible.

One shrugs and frowns
And says, "The hell with it,"
And dissolves slowly into
The fruit-cocktail for dinner.

The other cries softly
And collects its tears
In clear cider
With other disappointed lovers.

Man-made Mornings

Thomas Aud

Counter-top breakfasts of love,
reflected by eyeglasses and teacups.
Man hurrying off in his second-hand car
to attempt to stay off the mortgage menace.

Woman fighting for her own release
from oppression of others' liberation.
children, yet sexless in thoughts, yelling
for attention and thought food
and answers to non-philosophical questions
of why the world is and why not else.

Pets searching for their favorite toys
and for warm places in the light.
candid shots of lunar terrain
and landscapes littered with debris
of children's toys and adult castoffs.

Futuristic plans and thoughts
of two plus and of early morning
coming down from last night's love high.

BIO

Native Kentuckian, in Jackson since February 1975. Recently retired as Executive Director, Jackson/Madison County Library after over 31 years. Married, two children and one granddaughter. Developed an online course on libraries for Jackson State Community College. Hobbies: Geneology, Reading and Writing poetry, Sports Watching and Game Shows.

Only Once In A Life-Time

Dr. Clementine G. "Glem" Spencer

Only once in a life-time are we allowed to co-exist in a world, a place and time where hearts command where face to face love entwine…

Only once in a life-time are we allowed to cross a path that comes close to a taste of heaven on earth where happiness and joy combined with the real; where falseness, deception disappears…

Only once in a life-time do we find a song to sing that captures the meaning we desire; only once in a life-time are we allowed to set sail and anchor ourselves in a place where we are safe, loved and at peace…

Only once in a life-time are we allowed to reach out and be reached with endless strength, endless hope with no pursuant trails to follow, not for what is given, not what is received, but the one life-time you, the one of a kind friend, which there is no other…

BIO

Retired former teacher, presently teaches two nights at American Baptist College Ext-Jackson part-time RSVP Aide Meritan-Home Delivered Meals. Community Service Leader, Public Relations, Aid to Senior Citizens, Caregiver, Mother, Grandmother, 1967 Graduate of Lane College, Honorary Doctrate Tennessee School of Religion MPS. 1955 Graduate of Merry High School, and Gardner.

LIFE

Hyla Richardson

Life—that elusive magical thread that fastens each to earth
By its fragile strength so powerful which arrives with each at birth.

Life—that mystical unseen power that one can never hold,
For it is an intangible, yet it's more precious than gold.

Life. Did it come of its own volition, or was there a Creator Devine
Who wanted to fill the universe with creatures of His own design?

The spark of life that we hold dear and to keep it we constantly fight
Its many lurking enemies with a very tenacious might.

It is with us at the beginning and remains until the end.
We count it most precious as all components we blend.

Death, its triumphant foe awaits just a breath away
For that eternal ending—the final judgment day.

Me, Myself and I

Cassie McGill

Me is just alone
Myself is just alone in a group
I is just alone in the world
Is an empty part in her heart?
Me, myself, and I
Me, myself, and I is just one person that feels lonely
Who feels nobody cares
Who asks I'm I special?
Me, myself, and I
Can't say "she is beautiful"
What person makes me, myself, and I feel good?
But me, myself, and I figures out
She is not alone
She is distinctively special
And people really do care

BIO

My name is Cassie McGill. I live in Lexington, TN. I enjoy singing, hanging out with my friends, basketball, and writing. My love of writing developed by way of keeping a journal. I hope to one day have some of my writings published as well as become an author/journalist.

JOY...MUSIC OF THE SOUL

DORY LAMB

MAKE A JOYFUL NOISE
THE PSALMIST WOULD SAY
LIKE BIRDS IN FLIGHT
AND CHILDREN AT PLAY

A SMILE IS THE MUSIC
OF THE SOUL…
SHINING BRIGHT
A JOY TO BEHOLD

O TASTE AND SEE THAT
THE LORD IS GOOD
REJOICING RESULTS
FROM THE REDEEMERS FOOD

A PIECE OF CLAY
A TINY SEED BECOME
BEAUTIFUL THINGS
IN THE MASTERS HAND

MAKES A JOYFUL NOISE
THROUGHOUT THE LAND

BIO

Dory Lamb has been writing poetry since the early 80's. Her original works were mostly characatures as in "Seedlings." Her most recent is "Growing in Grace" and "The Fine Golden Thread." Her works are inspirational. Dory Lamb is a pseudonym. Her legal name is Doris Gilsdorf. Her older poems use her married name, Dolejs.

A STITCH IN TIME

DORY LAMB

FAITH IS LIKE A FINE GOLDEN THREAD
WEAVED INTO THE TAPESTRY OF LIFE
WON'T YOU STITCH ME A MOUNTAIN
WITH A CROSS ETCHED IN RED
AND SEW IN ONE GREEN, ON WHICH
SO MANY WERE FED...

WEAVE IN ONE WHITE DOVE
DESCENDING ON THE SAVIOR AND ONE
WITH AN OLIVE BRANCH WHICH TO
NOAHS EYE GAVE SUCH FAVOR

ALL THE COLORS OF THE RAINBOW
FROM THE GREAT I AM...
ADD ON THE GOLDEN MUSTARD SEED
AND THE FAITH OF ABRAHAM
WHERE IS THAT FISH THAT TAUGHT
JONAH A LESSON...

AND THOSE FISHERS- OF-MEN
FROM THAT TIME OF AGGRESSION
SKETCHED ON MY HEART AND
IN MY SOUL...
EACH COLOR A STORY...
SO NEW, YET SO OLD

Let the Bells Ring Loud

Erin Wyatt

Let the Bells ring loud!
And it takes away your mind-
Fills your world with sound
And killing sense of time.
Let the Bells ring loud!
Let them echo in your head
Pounding on your skull,
'Til time starts up again.
Let the Bells ring loud,
And it swallows us all whole,
Drowning us in sound
(True inside our heads.)
Let the Bells ring loud
Let them take away your mind;
Killing you with screams-
Let the Bells ring loud!
Let the storm-songs come-
With nothing in their way-
Calling out unearthly wrong
(In this world this day.
Let the Bells ring loud)
Warn that storm-songs come,
And there's no escape
From the truth that they are here.

~9/14/07

SHIVERING ON A MOUNTAINTOP

Sula Hillhouse

Shivering here in this makeshift tent
with my sisters and my dad;
my mother was taken from us
by the giant Tsunami our village had.

Night's darkness hovers 'round us;
we've no warm place to lay our heads.
Our meager possessions all washed away;
the hard, cold ground is our only bed.

Then suddenly appears a starlit sky
out of the blackness of this night.
Is someone up there to comfort me
and my family ~ all consumed by fright?

We are but worms in this vast unknown
and we just don't know what to do.
We're stranded alone on this jagged ridge
and of our location ~ no one has a clue.

Our fate is in the Master's hands
as we huddle together ~ trying to stay warm.
Each of us, in our own simple way,
asks God to send help when tomorrow dawns.

OUR PROMISED LAND

Sula Hillhouse

Come; walk along the shore with me
in silent contemplation.
There's no need to talk, you see;
thoughts are our conversation.

A great white bird glides near the surf;
its' message is of peace.
What happiness! Let's stop the world
so this joy will never cease.

A misty spray is barely felt.
Our world is fantasy.
There is but heaven in our hearts ~
and in life's mystery.

God grant that we shall never grow
too old to understand;
His Paradise is for us all.
It is our 'promised land'.

BIO

I grew up in Madison County, graduating from J B Young High School, West Tennessee Business College, and attending JSCC. My husband, Cecil Hillhouse, and I, have three daughters, five grandchildren and one great-grandchild. I retired from Jackson Surgical Associates, P.A. after 35 years in their employ.

A man was reaching for coffee, his hand suddenly became

David Strait

what he thought was like an animal, it's own legs
thundering under it, spreading deserts behind,
kicking up dust, chased by jeeps on safari,
by men with guns big as trees.

Was he the man on safari? He didn't remember,
but if he was, why
would he chase his own elephant?
And if it was his, why
did it look so distant,
so grey, and not at all like a hand?

And who was the other man
in the jeep, and which desert was this?
Why were they holding guns, and besides,
where was his coffee?

Birds? Sure,
I've got shelves full.

David Strait

See them lined up,
saddled, ready to fly?
Do you want to take one
for a ride?

The one I chose was yellow,
cold, and slightly
faded, a little old
but how that one could sing!

A good decision, yesssss…
he grinned, I reached
down in my pocket,
pulled out the largest coin.

No, no! a gift,
and this as well!
as he held out his hand,
palm up, with nothing, Here!

BIO

David Strait is in the final semester of Carlow University's MFA in Creative Writing. He has studied with Jan Beatty, Desmond Egan, and Michael Coady. He is working on his final manuscript for the MFA, supervised by Irish poet Mark Roper. Along with poetry, David writes short stories and drama.

Never Forgotten

Jeremy Elkins

Forevermore
The word itself
Echoes in my ears
Unleashed upon me
My darkest fears

Forevermore
Ever long, eternity
They fade
Then come back to me

I reach out to hold them
But it's just a dream
Then the day wakes me
Like blinding light
On a darkened screen

They fade
Then come back to me
If only for a while
They fade
Then come back to me
Allowing one more smile

For those few moments
The sun touches my face
My sadness dissipates
And with every breath
I taste the air
Reluctant to let it go

Forevermore
There's laughter and joy,
Sorrow and pain

Forevermore
Through summer winds
And winter rain
Hand in hand
The memories reside
Within my dreams
Forever

They fade
Then come back to me
Never forgotten

Tonight and Forever

Jeremy Elkins

I can see for miles in the moonlight
Then dawn arrives, so I must wait…

But tonight my love
I'll return to see you
Then by light my love
I will have freed you

Just a kiss
The tie that binds
Look in my eyes
Within my mind
Grasp my wings
And we will fly…
Tonight and forever

I've lived in darkness a thousand ages
To hold you in my arms at night…

The time has come
Turn back the pages
Together as one
Love won't betray us

Just a kiss
Love never dies
Trust your heart
To never lie
Take my wings
We'll fly together…
Tonight and forever

You'll be mine
No matter the cost
I will not have lost
Our love this time

You and I
Will make our destiny
We'll live eternally
Tonight and forever

BIO

Jeremy Elkins resides in Arlington, Tennessee with his wife, Maggie, and their many pets. He designs and builds custom furniture professionally and is a chef, musician, artist, as well as a lyricist and feels songs are merely poems put to music.

The Talent Among Us volumes are published locally by Main Street Publishing, Inc., located at 206 E. Main Street, Suite 207, Jackson, TN 38301.

For more information, contact Main Street Publishing at 1-866-457-7379 or email us at www.mainstreetpublishing.com

The Talent Among Us Volumes

Volume I   *Talent Among Us*

Volume II   *Poems & Short Stories*

Volume III   *Trail of Tales*

Volume IV   *Tracks in Time*

Volume V   *Pieces*

Volume VI   *Perceptions*

Volume VII   *Inspiration*

Order your copy today, call toll free **1-866-457-7379** *or order online at* **www.mainstreetpublishing.com**

Main Street Publishing, Inc.

206 E. Main Street Suite 207
P.O. Box 696
Jackson, Tn 38301

Toll Free #: 866-457-7379
or
Local #: 731-427-7379

Visit us on the web:
www.mainstreetpublishing.com
www.mspbooks.com

E-Mail: mspsupport@charterinternet.com